A.G.		M.L.		
Ans		MLW	5/03 Loretta	
Bev		Mt.Pl		
C.C.		NLM		
C.P.		Ott		
Dick		PC		
EC.H.		PH		
EC.S.		P.P.	11/03 10/07 Cam	
Gar	7/07	Pion.P.	2/04	
Gar.U.Pl.		Q.A.	6/04	
G.H.		Riv		
GRM	"/05 (AllA)	Ross	11/04	
GSA		S.C.		
GSP	"/06	St.A.		
G.V.	7/03	St.J		
Har		St.Joa		
JPCP		St.M.		
Jub		Sgt	4/06 (hilms)	
KEN	9/05 svekla	T.H.		
K.L.		T.M.		
K.M.		T.T.		
L.H.		Ven		
L.O.		Vets		
Lyn		VP		
L.V.	9/04 (Lil) 10/09	Wed		
McC		W.L.		
McG				
McQ				
R. Heiland	6/07			

CHANGE OF HEART

CHANGE OF HEART

Catherine Cross

Chivers Press • G.K. Hall & Co.
Bath, England   Waterville, Maine USA

This Large Print edition is published by Chivers Press, England, and by G.K. Hall & Co., USA.

Published in 2002 in the U.K. by arrangement with the author.

Published in 2002 in the U.S. by arrangement with Mary Cross.

U.K. Hardcover   ISBN 0–7540–4740–7 (Chivers Large Print)
U.K. Softcover   ISBN 0–7540–4741–5 (Camden Large Print)
U.S. Softcover   ISBN 0–7838–9668–9 (Nightingale Series Edition)

The text of this Large Print edition is unabridged.
Other aspects of the book may vary from the original edition.

Set in 16 pt. New Times Roman.

Printed in Great Britain on acid-free paper.

British Library Cataloguing in Publication Data available

Library of Congress Cataloging-in-Publication Data

Cross, Catherine, 1945–
 Change of heart / by Catherine Cross.
  p.   cm. — (G.K. Hall large print nightingale series)
 ISBN 0–7838–9668–9 (lg. print : sc : alk. paper)
 1. Caribbean Area—Fiction. 2. Large type books. I. Title.
II. Series.
PR6053.R598 C76 2002
823'.92—dc21   2001039975

CHAPTER ONE

She first noticed him as she swam in a lazy crawl towards the swimming platform. Despite the early hour, the clear, Caribbean water felt warm and silky against her skin, but it did nothing to lessen the tension building inside since her row with Gerald last night.

And now, the fair-haired stranger was in her favourite place, the swim already spoiled for her.

Approaching the platform, Nicky ignored the raft ladder, as usual, and started to haul herself out of the water. Halfway out, she was caught off-balance by a light swell and was thrown against the raft. As her leg hit the edge of the raft and pain knocked the breath from her, she lost her balance and fell back into the water.

Gasping out loud as she resurfaced, she knew that, despite her previous good intentions, she would need to rest for longer before beginning the swim back.

Hopefully, whoever was on the platform wouldn't start a conversation. Having to be polite was the last thing she felt like.

She pulled a face and knew she was probably being optimistic. Nicky attracted looks wherever she went. Her tall, lithe body and long, dark hair set off by dark-green eyes

1

made it impossible for people to ignore her. Although she had come to terms with it now, and was rarely aware of people's glances as they passed, she considered herself far from perfect.

This morning, she was wearing a one-piece swimsuit in a shimmering sea-green material which matched the colour of her eyes, and a ribbon in the same material caught the ends of the thick, single plait that hung down the centre of her back.

She made her way gingerly around to the ladder and pulled herself out of the water while trying to keep the weight off her injured leg.

Lowering herself gratefully on to the platform, she scowled at the bronzed, broad back the man presented to her. It must have been perfectly clear to him that someone else had joined him on the raft, yet he gave no indication of it.

Either he's deaf or totally rude, Nicky mused as she pressed her hand to her thigh in the hope of lessening the pain in her leg.

His thick hair was slicked back, curling in towards his neck and, as she continued to stare, powerful muscles rippled down his back, confirming to Nicky that he was aware of her presence.

Well, that suits me fine, she thought mutinously, forgetting that not many minutes ago she'd hoped he wouldn't start a

2

conversation.

She lowered her gaze, a startled cry tearing from her throat as cramp, more severe than the pain already in her leg, held her in its vice-like grip. Both hands went to her sun-tanned leg as she tried, in vain, to massage the pain away.

'Oh, no, please, not this,' she groaned, her eyes clouding.

The platform gave a lurch as the man rose to his feet and prepared to dive off into the clear, turquoise water. Nicky was briefly aware of broad shoulders, long, well-muscled legs and a pair of minuscule black briefs.

In other circumstances, she would have admired his clean entry into the water, but she could only view his departure with rising panic.

'Hey, you, stop! I need help,' she shouted as panic threatened to overwhelm her. She clenched her hands into fists. 'He's got to come back.'

She looked back at the beach and the palm trees that edged it, desperately searching for signs of life, but there were none. It would be hours before anyone discovered she was missing! If she wasn't at her desk by half past eight, the staff might think that she had gone into Bridgetown on an errand, especially as her walkie-talkie, which she carried everywhere with her, was still on her desk.

She bit her lip. Knowing she would be unable to swim back to the hotel unaided in her present state, she would have to swallow her pride and ask this stranger for help again.

If he was a guest from the hotel, he could swim back and get her father, or Gerald. No, on second thoughts, not Gerald.

The seconds ticked by like hours as she waited for some sign that he had heard her shouts. He stopped swimming and she shouted again.

'Help. Please, help.'

He turned and started to swim slowly back to the raft. As he approached, she wondered who he was. Hardly likely to be a guest from her father's hotel at this hour, so perhaps it was one of the crew from the large motor-cruiser anchored farther out in the bay.

'Drat the man. Why can't he go any faster?' she asked herself in an effort to take her mind off the pain.

She closed her eyes briefly and sighed in sheer relief. At least he was coming back. He stopped a few feet away from the raft and trod water.

'What's your problem?' he asked in a cold, unfriendly voice.

'I need help. I can't manage the swim back to the beach.'

He raised an eyebrow sardonically, his voice cutting across the water.

'Oh, really? You surprise me. You looked quite relaxed on the swim out. Very professional, in fact. You're not seriously expecting me to believe that you can't manage to get back, are you?'

Nicky, who had been taught by her mother to swim at the age of seven and had taken to it as easily as the flying-fish out in the bay, didn't know whether to be glad or annoyed that he had watched her swim out from the beach.

'If you're tired,' he continued, 'I suggest you rest up for a while before trying the return journey. There's nothing I can do about it.'

He began to turn away.

'No! Wait!' Desperation hardened her voice. 'I do need help.'

His exasperated sigh floated across the water to the raft.

'Give me one reason why.'

Nicky swallowed hard, containing the panic building in her.

'I've got cramp in my leg. It's very bad.'

She saw him frown and wondered whether he would still abandon her, but he headed for the ladder. Once on the raft, he looked about him before kneeling beside her.

'How did you manage this?' he asked, as he examined her leg, surprising Nicky with his gentleness. 'Well?' he asked again, when she didn't reply.

'I . . . um, I hit the side of the raft when I tried to get on to it. The swell caught me. I've never had cramp before when swimming so I can only think that the knock on my thigh started it.'

5

'Why didn't you use the ladder? Don't you know it can be dangerous getting on to one of these things?'

Nicky blushed to the roots of her hair. There was no need for him to remind her. Hadn't her mother, when she was alive, said the same thing to her many times before, when they used to swim out here together?

She pushed the thought away by keeping her eyes firmly on his head and shoulders during his examination.

'You'll live,' he said, raising piercing, pale-blue eyes to look at her.

She nodded, mesmerised by his eyes. They were surrounded by thick, dark lashes most women would kill for. Fine lines at the outer edges, the grooves lighter than the rest of his skin, made Nicky think that perhaps he spent a great deal of time outdoors, squinting against the sun. But what held her attention was the colour of his eyes. They reminded her of polar ice chips and looked twice as dangerous. She shivered.

'Cold?'

She shook her head slowly, so as not to aggravate the pain.

'I'd appreciate it if you could help me back to the beach now.'

'You from the hotel?'

'Yes.'

He looked at the waterproof Rolex chronometer strapped to his wrist, then back to the beach and out to the boat.

'Sorry, I can't do that. I don't have time. Anyway, the yacht is nearer.'

He stood up and held out a hand.

'Oh, but I can't do that. I have to get back.'

She looked towards the beach. Still no-one in sight.

'Why? Will the boyfriend be missing you?'

Nicky looked up at the stranger angrily.

'No! But I don't even know who you are, or anything about you. Give me one reason why I should come with you?' she said.

He racked a hand through his wet hair and gave an exasperated sigh.

'What's to know? You need help, and it looks like I'm all that's available. Either you let me help you, or you get back to the hotel under your own steam. Make up your mind because I'm going now, with or without you.'

He turned his back as if to move away.

Frightened of the consequences if he left her, Nicky tried to drag herself to her feet.

'No! I'm coming.'

In her desire not to be left behind, she had risen too quickly, and the pain which threatened to swamp her sent her crashing to her knees.

The stranger turned around and stared down at her, unconsciously steadying himself against the slight movement of the platform on the water's swell. He helped her to stand and put his hands on her shoulders to steady her as she balanced precariously on her good leg.

'Do you know anything about life-saving procedures?'

'Yes,' she said between clenched teeth.

'Fine. When we get into the water, do exactly as I tell you. If you don't, I'll leave you where you are and you can get back the best way you can. No panicking or fighting me, is that understood?'

She nodded, biting hard on her bottom lip. The man's an arrogant, insufferable bighead, but what choice do I have, she thought angrily.

The stranger eased her into the water and the cold made her cramp worse, the pain shooting down to her ankle, making Nicky feel more panic-stricken than ever. She was hardly aware of the short journey to the yacht or of being carried up the bathing ladder at the stern of the vessel, in a fireman's lift.

She was taken to a small cabin and laid gently on the bed. The walls were panelled in Bird's-eye maple and the curtains at the small window and the bedspread on which she was lying were made with a dark blue, russet and gold fabric. A thick, off-white carpet covered the small floor space.

The stranger had started to massage her leg, when a large, elderly gentleman in white slacks and shirt and a peaked, blue sailor's cap came into the room. The sleeves of his shirt were rolled up to reveal strong, hair-covered arms.

The stranger worked as he talked to the

8

other man and snatches of their conversation drifted over to her.

'. . . bimbo from the hotel . . . couldn't see a photographer . . . looked like a setup.'

None of it made much sense to Nicky. She concentrated on him. A scattering of dark hairs on his chest tapered down to slim hips and long legs. She could have stayed there all day looking at him. She shook her head. The pain, although receding, must be addling her brain, she decided, contemplating a complete stranger in that way.

The two men stopped talking and exchanged a glance. The elderly man looked at Nicky and smiled. When he spoke it was in a strong, American accent.

'Well, hello there, little lady. How are you feeling now?'

She blinked at him, lost for words. Standing five foot ten in her bare feet, Nicky couldn't remember the last time someone had called her 'little.' She laughed, and once started could not seem to stop.

Her shoulders were grabbed by strong fingers which bit into her flesh, and she was shaken violently.

'Stop it! Stop it now!'

She looked up at impenetrable, blue eyes which suddenly seemed too close for safety. She closed her own tightly and sighed, embarrassed at her outburst.

She heard the American say, 'Jack, don't

9

you think you are being too hard on her?'

'No. She's probably in shock. She must get back to the hotel as soon as possible and see a doctor.'

He turned to her.

'Has the pain gone now?'

Nicky could only nod, as a single, hot tear escaped and slid down her cheek. He finished massaging her leg to his obvious satisfaction.

'Go and find something to wrap her in, Mike.'

The big man was soon back with a large, fluffy towelling robe for Nicky which he proceeded to help her into. She had started to shiver and was glad of the robe. She pulled the belt tight around her waist and thought she caught a faint smell of citrus as she turned back the sleeves to a more suitable length.

'Thank you.'

'You're welcome, little lady,' he said as he left the cabin.

Jack had pulled on a pair of jeans over his trunks. He now slipped his feet into a pair of canvas loafers, turned to the cabin door and opened it.

'Let's get you back. I've wasted enough time already.'

Her relief was short-lived and she bristled at his comment.

'Charming! I can assure you that . . .'

'Save your breath. You can have your say on the way back.'

10

He left the cabin and there was nothing for it but for Nicky to follow him, still fuming. Why did he have to be so rude to her? It wasn't her fault that she had cramp!

How did I manage to end up getting rescued by probably the most obnoxious man on the island, she wondered. As far as I'm concerned, if I never see him again, it'll be too soon for me!

She followed him out to a hall panelled entirely in Bird's-eye maple. Her eyes opened in amazement. The fittings on this boat were sumptuous. She hadn't been aware of them when she came on board, but having helped her father completely refurbish their hotel just two years ago, she was well aware of the sort of money needed to fit out a boat to such a high standard.

She thought, idly, that Mike must have a lot of money to be able to keep a boat like this. Jack took her up the carpeted stairs, through the main saloon and dining area, and slid open a large, glass door. She followed him out on to the aft cockpit.

Nicky was surprised to find that the sun was already quite high in the sky and the deck was warm to her bare feet. She heard the hum of an electric winch as Mike lowered the dinghy to the water.

'Here, give me your hand, my dear,' he said, and helped Nicky negotiate the bathing ladder to get into the little boat. 'We'll have you back

11

in no time.'

He started to follow, but Jack put out a restraining hand and climbed down to the dinghy himself.

'I'll go, Mike.'

'But Jack, I thought—' the American started.

'Yes, I know, but it can't be helped. You will just have to call Hong Kong for me. Speak to Emerald and tell her I've been held up.'

He started the dinghy's outboard engine and cast off.

'Fax that pile of papers on my desk through to her and tell her to call me when she has had time to read them. I'll be back in about twenty minutes.'

The short journey was made in silence. Nicky knew she should be grateful to Jack for helping her, but he made it so obvious she was just a pain in the neck. She wished he didn't make her so angry.

She glanced quickly at Jack sitting in the stern. He was looking straight ahead, his expression unreadable. In profile, his face looked all angles and planes—high cheekbones, square jaw.

She snuggled down in the towelling robe, pulling it more tightly around her, once more aware of the delicate lemon smell which seemed to permeate the cotton material. She wondered, briefly, who owned it. Although feeling better by the minute now she had no

12

pain, she was nevertheless glad of the robe as she still felt cold and shaky.

They were nearing land and Nicky shielded her eyes against the glare of the sun which bounced back off the surface of the water. She could see people walking along the beach, some settling themselves on loungers under huge sun umbrellas, oiling their bodies in readiness of the day's roasting. A few energetic souls were even splashing around in the shallows.

Jack cut the engine as the little boat coasted in towards the beach and Nicky braced herself for the jolt as the prow hit the white sand. Jumping out of the boat and pulling it up the beach a few feet, Jack then turned his attention to Nicky and helped her out.

She sighed with relief as her toes dug into the powdery sand but her euphoria was short-lived as she was swung off her feet unceremoniously and held in powerful arms.

'Put me down,' she burst out, trying unsuccessfully to wriggle free.

Jack, ignoring her effort to escape, started to walk up the beach with her in his arms.

'This really isn't necessary, you know,' she said. 'I'm quite capable of walking on my own.'

'I'm sure you are, but I don't think we should take any risks with the leg.'

People on the beach were beginning to stare at them.

'Oh, yes? And what risk would that be?'

13

He shifted her to a more comfortable position.

'There's a risk that the cramp may start again if you have to strain your muscles by walking over this soft sand. Be a good girl and put your arms around my neck. It'll make it easier for both of us.'

'Who are you kidding?' she said, looking at him warily.

The look he gave her was one of pure innocence.

'Try it. You might be surprised.'

Convincing herself that it was easier to go with the tide than argue, Nicky slid her hands over his sun-warmed shoulders and across his back. Her fingers tingled as they touched his smooth skin and it seemed entirely natural to lay her head on his shoulder.

He carried her past the palm-fringed edge of the beach, through the tamarind trees and on to the lawns of the hotel garden, skirting thick clumps of lantanas and brightly-coloured hibiscus.

Nicky didn't notice. The events of the morning and the warmth of the sun had eventually caught up with her. Everything seemed different, somehow, even her behaviour.

Her world shrunk until it consisted only of Jack's shoulders and back. She breathed in deeply. The fresh, masculine smell of him was intoxicating, overlaid as it was by the elusive citrus smell which she had noticed on the robe. So, it was Jack's robe she was wearing! She hugged the thought happily to herself. She smiled against his skin and felt him tense.

'Stop that, you witch.'

'Stop what, Jack?' she breathed.

He gave a warning growl. She knew she shouldn't be teasing him, a complete stranger, but he seemed to bring out the devil in her.

It was like playing with a sleeping tiger. As long as it slept, you were safe. When it woke up, you had to jump clear, and she wasn't sure she wanted to be around when this particular tiger woke up.

He carried her across the terrace, where large, terracotta pots overflowed with brightly-coloured blossoms, orange and blue strelitzias, looking for all the world like the birds of paradise they were said to resemble, and on into the hotel. The marble reception hall cooled her skin—and her nerve. The tiger was about to wake up. She shivered.

Her legs were unsteady as Jack lowered her gently to the ground.

'And now,' he said, as he slid his arms around her and tightened his grip. 'I shall need payment for services rendered this morning.'

Nicky leaned back and looked up at him, confused.

'Payment?'

He nodded slowly. She saw the subtle change of expression in his eyes, but was

15

totally unprepared for what happened.

His mouth came down on hers possessively, demanding a response. It was all Nicky could do to keep her feet. Her hands moved to his shoulders and clung to him. He tasted of sea spray and Nicky suddenly wanted nothing more than to stay there, locked in his arms for ever. A voice penetrated her muddled brain.

'And what, exactly, do you think you are doing with my fiancée?'

She froze. It was Gerald! She tried to untangle herself from Jack's embrace, but he was too quick. He moved one hand up to support her head, deepening the kiss. She opened her eyes in amazement when he released her slowly. Now her legs definitely wouldn't support her. She held on to the reception desk.

'Well? I'm waiting for an answer!'

The sandy-haired man moved towards them, bristling with anger. Nicky couldn't think of a thing to say and, what was worse, her tongue seemed to be glued to the roof of her mouth. She looked from one man to the other.

'This is your fiancée?' Jack said, pushing his hands into the pockets of his jeans.

'Yes, she is!'

'No, I'm not!' Nicky declared, suddenly finding her voice.

Who did Gerald think he was? There had never been anything between them, except,

16

perhaps, wishful thinking on Gerald's part, and after the row last night there never would be.

Jack raised an eyebrow and smiled grimly.

'Then if I were you, I'd take better care of my property.'

'Now just hang on there a minute,' Nicky argued, 'I'm not anybody's property.'

But she was speaking to thin air. Jack had already pushed through the plate-glass doors and was striding away across the terrace towards the beach.

CHAPTER TWO

Nicky turned on Gerald as soon as they were alone in her office. She stood in the middle of the floor, clenching and unclenching her hands in an effort to hold on to her temper.

'What exactly did you mean by that? Saying we were engaged?'

'Now, Nicky, don't get upset.'

He walked towards her and caught her hands in his.

'I just wanted to help. I thought you were in trouble and needed rescuing.'

'You thought I was in trouble?' Her voice rose half an octave. 'Whatever gave you that idea?'

She pulled free of his hands and went to stand by her desk, pulling the robe tight around her neck.

He shrugged his shoulders.

'Well, there you were, being mauled by a complete stranger. I thought he was making unwelcome advances.' He gestured towards the towelling robe. 'And you aren't even properly dressed, so naturally I thought you were in trouble.'

'Hang on a minute. I was not being mauled, as you put it, and who says he was a complete stranger?'

Gerald had the grace to look flustered. He moved towards Nicky and put his hands on her shoulders.

'Nicky, you know how I feel about you.'

She sighed. 'Gerald, don't let's go over old ground again. You know there can never be anything more than friendship between us.'

His pale skin, scatted with freckles, turned paler.

'Look, I know what you said last night, but I think you should think again, or at least give yourself some time to consider it.'

'There's nothing to think about. Since you came here as manager for my father six years ago,' Nicky said, 'we've worked well together. I've enjoyed your company. Don't let's spoil it.'

She had tried to let him down gently the night before, but he was beginning to annoy her now.

'But, Nicky—'

'No! I've said all I'm going to say. Besides,

18

I'm not the slightest bit interested in marriage, as I've already told you. Since Pops had his heart attack last year, he has been my main concern. The extra responsibilities I have taken on wouldn't leave much time for marriage.'

He looked at her sceptically, his wide mouth thinning to a narrow line.

'Are you seriously expecting me to—'

'I'm not expecting you to do or say anything, Gerald. Just back off,' she finished, and left the office to go to her own cottage to get dressed.

*   *   *

The party was in full swing when Nicky arrived, and, apart from a slight ache in her leg, she felt totally relaxed and looking forward to the evening ahead. She was wearing a cream figure-hugging dress covered with diamante and tiny seed pearls. The dress rustled sensuously against her legs as she moved and the diamante caught the light of the coloured lanterns placed at strategic points around the garden and in the trees.

This was the party her father held each year to mark his ownership of the hotel. Her mother had suggested it at the end of their first year, inviting the few new friends they had made, until this year, their twenty-first anniversary, there were nearly a hundred

19

friends gathered to help them celebrate.

Her father liked to continue the tradition even after his wife's death, and Nicky, after finishing her schooling in England, was happy to act as hostess.

Picking up a glass of champagne from a passing waiter's tray, she looked around, smiling at the guests, all of whom she had come to know over the years. She would mingle later, but for the moment, she just gazed around the crowd.

Her eyes caught on a handsome face. One particular man stood slightly apart from the crowd, staring straight at her. He was dressed as every other man present, but his clothes fitted him so superbly they set him in a class apart. An aura of calm serenity radiated from him and she watched as he slowly raised his glass to salute her. As recognition dawned, the smile left her face and her heart missed a beat.

Jack! Here? She couldn't believe it! Why was he here, gatecrashing? It was one thing to help a person in trouble, but that didn't mean they could just waltz into private parties unannounced, drinking other people's champagne.

She wondered if his boss, the yacht owner, knew where he was. Bristling with indignation, she left her glass on a nearby table and marched across to him.

'How did you get in?' she demanded, coming to a stop in front of him.

'Well, good-evening, yourself.'

He smiled at her and swallowed a long draught of champagne.

'This is a private party. You're gatecrashing.'

'Am I?' He kept his smile in place. 'Now, what sort of welcome is that, for the rescuer of a damsel in distress?'

Nicky bit her lip. She had to admit he did have a point, but the embarrassing memory of Gerald discovering them locked in each other's arms stood out in her mind. No, Jack had a lot to answer for.

She tossed her head angrily, sending her thick, dark hair swirling over her bare shoulders to settle again in waves down her back.

'You will have to leave,' she persisted.

'Why?'

'Because . . . because I say so.'

'No.'

'You mean you're not going?' she said, her eyes wide open in amazement.

'That's right.'

'Then I'll get the security guards to remove you.'

'OK.'

She looked at him, puzzled.

'You want me to get the guards?'

'If that's what you want.'

'Right. If that's your last word, I will.'

Nicky turned to leave, but he was too quick.

A hand snaked out and held her wrist in a grip of steel.

'When you send the security guards, remember to tell them whom you want to throw out. Tell them Jack Morgan.'

She turned and ran, his rich, dark laugh ringing out after her across the grass.

'Damn you, Jack Morgan,' she stormed as she ran. 'I'll get rid of you, see if I don't.'

CHAPTER THREE

Nicky ran as though the devil himself were after her, Jack's laughter ringing in her head every step of the way.

She tracked her father down in the library, sitting at his desk, studying some papers. She smiled at him affectionately as she crossed the room to drop a kiss on the top of his head. Although now in his mid-fifties, he was still a handsome man and carried himself well, despite his recent heart attack.

'Why aren't you outside enjoying yourself, young lady?' he asked, smiling back at her.

'We've got a gatecrasher and I want you to get rid of him.'

A knock on the open door behind her made her turn around. She gave an involuntary gasp as she saw Jack Morgan staring straight at her. He had followed her! But why?

She turned to look at her father. David Kington was walking towards the open door, smiling.

'Jack, it's good to see you again. Come on in,' he invited, moving towards his guest.

The two men shook hands.

'I don't think you have met my daughter, Nicky, have you?'

'Yes.'

'No!' Nicky blurted out at the same time.

Her father laughed. Nicky cleared her throat, not knowing where to start or even if she could. As usual, Jack had put her in an awkward position and she felt sure he was enjoying every minute of it. He wasn't making this easy for her. Jack spoke first.

'I did meet your daughter briefly, David, but she didn't introduce herself. I think she had other things on her mind at the time.'

She couldn't believe what she was hearing. The sheer audacity of the man made Nicky want to lash out at him, but she bit down on an angry retort, realising that if they started arguing in front of her father, he would never believe they were comparative strangers.

The ringing of the telephone broke the atmosphere in the room. David took the call. When he replaced the receiver, his face was grim.

'You'll have to excuse me, Jack. One of our friends has had an accident and I must see what I can do.'

He turned to Nicky.

'I think you should go and mingle, darling. I'm sure Jack will be all right here on his own for a while.'

I'm sure he will, Nicky thought as her father left the room hurriedly. If Pops thinks I'm leaving Jack on his own, he's got another think coming! He could be up to anything while we were away. He isn't safe to have around.

'Nice weather for the time of year, isn't it?' she said, hoping to bore him into silence with some inane chatter.

Her smile was sweetness itself as she lowered herself to the sofa. She knew she should have asked him to take a seat but, still smarting over their earlier encounters, she squashed the idea. She was fast discovering that whenever Jack Morgan appeared, her manners disappeared.

He laughed, as though he knew what she was attempting, and walked across the polished, wood floor, to make himself comfortable in a leather chair. Balancing his right ankle on his left knee and resting his elbows on the arms of the chair, he made a pyramid of his forearms and hands and looked at her over the top of it.

'Trusting, little soul, aren't you?' he said.

'About as trusting as you, I'd say,' she retorted, giving him a look which, seen by a lesser man, would have quelled any further conversation.

He smiled. Nicky wished he wouldn't do that. It made her legs go weak and she felt the urge to smile right back.

She pulled herself together. Anger. That was the thing. She must concentrate on it. Then it would form a shell around her and protect her from these other feelings.

'So,' he said, his eyes taking in the elegant bookcases which lined the walls of the library, with their leather-bound contents, 'what do you and your father plan to do with the money?'

She raised her eyebrows enquiringly.

'What do we plan to do with what money?'

'The money raised from the sale of this hotel, of course.'

She frowned. 'I don't know where you got your information from, but I can assure you that my father has absolutely no intention of selling this hotel.'

She narrowed her eyes angrily, her pulse quickening. Wherever had he got that particular piece of misinformation from, she wondered. If the rumour spread it could do untold damage to the hotel's reputation and profits. People would stay away, and it had not been a particularly good year so far for tourists.

'If I were you, Mr Morgan, I would stop spreading inaccurate and scandalous rumours before someone sues you for slander. I shall tell my father about this when he comes back.'

25

Jack watched her intently. His brows drew together and blue eyes pierced hers, his face a mask. Finally he spoke.

'No slander, Miss Kington, I assure you. I am here this evening to finalise arrangements and sign the papers. When I have signed, this hotel and everything in it will be mine.'

Nicky was on her feet in a trice.

'If you think I'm going to stay here and listen to your lies, you're wrong,' she stormed.

Her hands clenched and unclenched at her sides. Her mind was numb and she felt cold, as though icicles were clawing at her heart.

'My father would never sell without telling me, and we haven't even discussed it. You're trying to cause mischief for some reason or another. I don't know why, but I won't be a party to it!'

She turned to leave the room, but he was on his feet in an instant and reached the door first, his hand forcing it shut.

'You're not going anywhere just yet.'

'Oh, yes, I am,' Nicky raged at him, her voice shaking with emotion. 'Get out of my way.'

She tried to push past him and open the door, but he was too strong for her. He clamped his hands around her wrists and dragged her back into the room.

'Let go of me this instant,' she gasped, thrashing her arms about in an effort to break his grip.

It was like trying to break out of steel handcuffs. She thought ruefully of the bruises which would appear tomorrow.

'I'll let you go when you have calmed down,' he said, forcing her hands behind her back and pulling her towards him until she was trapped against his body.

His eyes, now just inches from hers, moved slowly over every part of her face, as though memorising each tiny detail.

He was angry, but somehow she didn't think his anger was directed at her. The icy chips seemed to thaw slightly as she gazed back at him.

'Your father tells me he has suffered a heart attack recently,' he went on.

His voice, soft now, soothed her. She nodded.

'And do you think that now, whilst he is so worried about his friend, it would do him any good to have you storming after him?'

In spite of her anger, the corners of her mouth quirked up at the thought. No, she supposed, it probably wouldn't. She had agreed, although reluctantly.

'No,' she whispered.

'I didn't hear your answer.'

'No,' she said, louder.

'Good, now we are getting somewhere. And do you also understand that what I have told you is the truth?'

She closed her eyes and sighed. His words

had a terrible ring of truth about them. Her father rarely discussed important issues with Nicky, still considering her to be his baby, and not a young woman of twenty-six.

'Yes.'

It was all too much for her. The proximity of him, the shock she had just had, all conspired against her and her legs buckled.

He lifted her in his arms, carried her over to the sofa and deposited her gently amongst the cushions. Then, finding the drinks trolley, he unstoppered several cut-crystal decanters, inhaling their contents, until he found the brandy.

He poured a large measure and brought it back to Nicky. After helping her to get comfy, he sat down beside her and handed her the glass.

'Drink this.'

She sniffed it and pulled a face, but downed half the contents before handing him back the glass. Then she lay back against the cushions and closed her eyes.

'Why didn't he tell me, Jack?'

'You will have to ask him that question yourself. All I can tell you is that he approached me some months ago with the idea. He was over-budget refurbishing the hotel, and at about the same time, he made some bad investments. They are just coming home to roost now. This was confirmed when I looked at the hotel's books.' He turned to look at her. 'You didn't have any idea?'

She shook her head.

'No. Pops has always taken care of the financial side of the business. Mind you, he has seemed pre-occupied recently, but when I asked him if he had any problems he said no.'

'Under normal circumstances,' Jack explained, 'these things could have been weathered, in time, but taken with the lack of tourism the islands have had these past few years . . .'

Nicky could hardly take in what he was saying. It was unthinkable that very shortly she would have to leave the hotel which had been her home for most of her life and, possibly, even the island, which she had loved since she was a child.

She wanted to hate Jack for all the hurt she was feeling. She wanted to blame him, too, for his part in all this but she knew in her heart that if it hadn't been Jack, it would have been someone else.

Tears escaped from under long, dark lashes but she refused to give in to them and dashed them away angrily with the back of her hand.

'But, who are you and, more to the point, why are you determined on buying the hotel if, as you say, things aren't too good?'

'I already own three hotels on the islands,' he said, naming three prestigious hotels on St Lucia, Nevis and Antigua.

Nicky knew the hotels he named and was

impressed.

'One on Barbados would be perfect, especially this one. Although things are tough just now, I feel that your father's business only needs some cash to weather this particular squall and a firm hand on the helm to keep it steady for a while before things improve. Your father just happens to be cash-poor at the moment. I also invest in the stock market and recently things have been good for me.'

'And are you any good at it? Playing the stock market?' she asked.

'Some people say I've got a nose for it.'

Hm, Nicky thought, acidly, wouldn't you just know it! He owns hotels that make money, plays the stock market and wins—the man's probably perfect! She was getting more bad-tempered by the minute.

'Why on earth didn't he tell me?' she persisted. 'We could have worked out something between us, I'm sure. If, as you say, we just need some more money to tide us over, we could make economies for a while, perhaps get an extra loan from the bank. It can't really be necessary to sell out to you.'

'You don't know what you're saying. The figure he needs runs into millions of dollars, not a few thousand.'

Nicky swallowed hard.

'Millions?' she asked, astonished.

'Better he lets me buy it, then he knows that the standards will be kept up. This hotel means a lot to him.'

'What do you know about it?' Nicky asked bitterly. 'This is his life. He doesn't know anything else. If you take my father away from the hotel, you take away his will to live. And where could he live? He won't be able to stay on the island knowing someone else is running his pride and joy. It doesn't matter for me. I can always find a job, but for Pops it's different.'

Jack's face hardened.

'Your father will come out of this deal very well, financially.'

'Big deal,' she replied. 'I suppose that's supposed to solve everything. Well, it doesn't! Just because money is your god, it doesn't mean everyone else has the same standards.'

Her eyes flashed and she wanted desperately to slap his face. But he gripped her shoulders, his fingers biting deep into her flesh.

'You don't know the first thing about me. How could you possibly know what I feel about anything, least of all this?'

'But now you do know about my father, you're still going to buy it from under him,' she said, her voice rising.

'For goodness' sake, woman, this is business.'

'If that's business, I don't want any part of it. And stop shouting at me,' she shouted back.

Nicky could see the fight he was having to

keep his temper. He was quiet for a very long time, but when he spoke next, he had lowered his voice.

'Then I won't buy!'

Nicky's mouth dropped open. The enormity of what she had done hit her. Even though her father had not discussed it with her, he obviously needed to sell. He had also found a buyer that he felt was suitable, for hadn't he approached Jack himself? Now, all on her own, she had opened her mouth, put both feet in and probably ruined everything for him.

'Shut your mouth! You look like a fish that's just been landed,' he said.

She closed her mouth, then opened it again immediately.

'So you're not going to buy after all? That's just great! What will happen to us now?'

'Saints preserve us!' Jack muttered under his breath. 'You can't have it all ways. Either you want to sell, or you don't. Besides, your father has already agreed.'

Nicky covered her face with her hands. Why can't I just shut up instead of always wanting to needle him? Anyway, she convinced herself, it's his fault for always irritating me.

She felt his weight on the sofa beside her again and he gently pulled her hands away.

'I won't buy. I've got a better idea, you see.'

She stared at him suspiciously.

'What?'

'A partnership. I'll put up the money needed

32

to keep the hotel going and it will be run on my terms. Your father will keep his will to live, as you put it, and I will still get a good investment.'

'That's fine,' Nicky said, 'but what about me?'

Jack's smile was predatory and his eyes held hers, demanding her submission. Her throat was suddenly dry and she swallowed hard. She didn't think she was going to like his answer.

Jack raised his hand to touch her face and slowly, very slowly, moved a finger down the side of her face, under her jaw, down the slender column of her throat, to stop in the hollow at its base.

'Oh, I'm sure I'll think of something.'

CHAPTER FOUR

The next morning, Nicky fumbled for the cut-off button on the alarm clock which was summoning her from an exhausted sleep. She opened one eye and groaned. Only four hours since she had fallen into bed in the early hours of the morning!

She dragged herself out of bed and headed for the shower, knowing that if she lay mulling over the events of the night she would never get up.

Jack had only stayed long enough to see

David and tell him about his new idea. Nicky couldn't help but be delighted as her father thanked the younger man profusely.

Jack had held up his hand and said, 'I think you should wait until you hear my terms before thanking me, David. I'll go back to the yacht now and work out some details. I'll call you first thing, and we can discuss it. Oh, by the way, how is the friend?'

'On his way to hospital. He missed his footing going down the steps into the garden. Looks like he's broken his leg. Nothing more serious, though, thank goodness.'

'Talking of things serious,' Jack said, 'I think it would be best if the two of you had a good night's sleep before any discussions on the future of the hotel.'

He looked pointedly at Nicky. He was right, of course. It wouldn't have been wise to start a conversation with her father that might go on for hours. He was beginning to look tired already. Besides, they still had a party to go to. She nodded.

'Good. Well, I'll be in touch, David,' he said, shaking the older man's hand. He smiled briefly at her. 'Good-night.'

His consideration for her father was a big surprise to Nicky. She imagined that a high-powered businessman like Jack would only be interested in the balance sheet and not the person. It looked as if she might have to change her opinion of him.

She was fair-minded enough to realise that even if he tangled her emotions and left her wanting to scream at him whenever they met, there was more to him than she had first thought. She sighed. Now she was even beginning to like the man!

Nicky and her father spent the next few hours mingling with their friends. Her father, although tired, looked ecstatically happy; Nicky managed to keep going on a mixture of adrenaline and champagne!

That's probably the reason I can't get going this morning, Nicky thought, soaping her body under the warm jets of water.

After dressing carefully in a skirt which swirled about her legs, and a long-sleeved shirt to cover the bruises which had, predictably, appeared on her wrists and shoulders, she went in search of her father, finally tracking him down in his suite of rooms at the top of the hotel. He was propped up in bed eating breakfast, something he had taken to doing since his heart attack.

'There you are, my darling, come on in,' he said, waving a piece of toast at her. 'Do you want some breakfast?'

'No thanks, Pops.'

She kissed his cheek and sat down on the edge of the bed, delighted to see that he looked as happy this morning as he had last night. He looked at her shrewdly.

'Mmm, I'm ordering you some anyway. You

35

look decidedly peaky.'

He picked up the phone, dialled room service and ordered.

'That's great,' she said, laughing at him. 'I look peaky but you look like the cat who's found a bowl full of cream.'

He smiled, spooning marmalade on to a fresh piece of toast.

'I must admit, my dear, that I feel wonderful this morning. What a perfect answer to our situation. A partnership. What ever made Jack think of that, I wonder.'

His eyes questioned Nicky. She dropped her gaze and fiddled with the bedspread.

'I've no idea,' she lied.

'Well, whatever the reason, at least now we won't have to leave, and for that I will be eternally grateful. It would have been a terrible wrench, you know.' She nodded. 'Jack has some wonderful ideas for the hotel. We have had a long talk on the phone already this morning.'

Watching her father as he chatted on about the hotel's future, Nicky wondered how she had missed seeing what a worry it must have been to him. It was all too easy to ignore the small changes that crept over people, day after day, but today he was so different, so happy, just like he used to be when her mother was alive.

'Nicky.'

'Mmm?' She stopped day-dreaming.

He looked at her sheepishly.

'Nicky, I owe you an apology for not telling you about the intended sale.'

She started to speak, but he waved her to silence.

'No, hear me out.'

He poured more coffee and settled back against his pillows.

'I had planned to tell you yesterday, but what with everything else . . .' He shrugged. 'Anyway, you now know some of the reasons why I had to do it.'

'Yes, Jack told me last night about the refurbishing costs and the bad investments.'

'Everything came at once. Those things, plus my heart attack. When you took on so much more responsibility, it worried me that you would end up an old maid with the hotel around your neck, never having the love and support of a family of your own. I was afraid that you would work yourself into the ground without giving your private life a chance.'

'But, Pops—'

'No, Nicky.' He smiled gently at her. 'I knew then that I was being selfish, and had to do something positive before we lost everything. I won't always be here for you but now, with luck, when I die, you will either have the option to stay as partner with Jack or take the money and do what you want. At least you will be protected, just like I always tried to protect your mother.'

37

Nicky saw tears form in his eyes and leaned over to hug him. She could forgive him anything right now. The terrible hurt she had felt the previous night at being excluded from his decision had lessened in the face of his happiness and his reason for doing it.

'Oh, Pops, I know you've always done the right thing for us,' she said huskily as they kissed each other.

'The last thing I wanted was for you to find out from someone else, but I hope you can forgive me, Nicky.'

'There's nothing to forgive,' Nicky said, mentally crossing her fingers and praying that her father would find Jack to be everything he needed.

Besides, there was nothing to do now but make the best of it. A knock on the door heralded the arrival of Nicky's breakfast and, as she ate, she encouraged David to talk about the future.

'Jack says we are to carry on as usual until he comes back, and he is transferring money to our current account at the bank this morning.' He beamed.

Nicky looked at her father in surprise.

'But you two only agreed on a partnership last night. You can't have seen a contract yet, have you?' Nicky asked.

'Of course not. It'll take a while to draw one up, I expect,' her father said, 'but we'll get one, don't worry.'

'And he's putting money into the hotel's account without anything in writing?'

'Well, yes, but he can trust me, Nicky.'

'That's all very well for you to say, but what do we know about him?'

Her father frowned at her.

'We know he runs three of the best hotels on the islands, for a start. What more do you need to know?'

Nicky shrugged.

'He must have a personal life.'

She missed the glimmer of a smile that passed over David's face at her question.

'All I know is that he lives on his yacht and runs his businesses from there. He says it allows him to keep his finger on the pulse of every hotel without having an office in each. Seems like a good idea to me. Pity I hadn't had an idea like that when your mother was alive. Whether or not he is married, I can't say. He seems to be a very private person.'

So much for my idea that he was nothing more than someone else's employee, Nicky thought wryly.

She felt uneasy though. A man like Jack would never put money into someone else's account without watertight contacts. He must be up to something, but what? She made up her mind to find out.

*　　　*　　　*

39

Jack eventually showed up two weeks later. They had been two weeks of frustrated, nail-biting tension for Nicky, who swung from desperately wanting to see him to not caring if she never saw him again—usually within the space of the same hour!

As it turned out, it was the lull before the storm. He whirled into the hotel like an out-of-season hurricane, scattering staff and instructions in all directions.

Nicky couldn't fault his professionalism. As soon as he arrived, he organised a meeting with her father and asked her to attend.

'These are the plans that I would like to see implemented here,' he said, handing each of them folders packed with closely-typed sheets of paper. 'I would like to go through them all with you now, if you have time, and then get your views.'

They spent the next two hours discussing each idea individually. When Jack had finished, her father wore a rather bemused expression and Nicky was quietly excited. He had some good ideas and she was longing to put them into practice. He was brisk and business-like.

'Nicky, when I've had a chat with your father, could you spare me some time in, say, twenty minutes?'

'Of course.'

'Good. I'll come down to your office.'

His brief smile touched his mouth but not

40

his eyes and he turned towards her father as though dismissing her from his mind. The excitement of seeing him again drained away and she felt as though she had been slapped in the face.

Back in her office, she idly turned over a few papers on her desk, unable to settle. He had seemed so cold and aloof. And why not, she thought. She was only an employee of his now, nothing more.

Her defences were obviously low where he was concerned. She would have to make sure that, in future, she tried to avoid him unless absolutely necessary. She realised, with a heavy heart, that it was going to be difficult. Just then the object of her thoughts came into her office.

'I did knock, but there was no reply,' he said as he walked towards her.

'What? Oh, sorry. I must have been day-dreaming.'

She tried a smile, but he didn't smile back as he sat down opposite her.

'What are your honest views of the plans, Nicky. Not what you think I want to hear, but the truth.'

'Whenever you ask me something, I will always give you an honest answer,' she replied stiffly, hurt that he thought she would be anything less than honest with him. 'You might not like it, but it will be the truth as I see it. I like the plans and I think the hotel will benefit enormously from them.'

'You can climb down off that horse you're on right now,' he ordered. 'We are going to be working together, hopefully, for years, so we might just as well get the foundations for a good, working relationship in place now, don't you think?'

Working together for years? Just the thought of it made Nicky feel weak, but how would she cope with seeing him frequently and only being viewed as an employee? Getting to know his wife and family, if he had one, and seeing them together would put a strain on her emotions, she realised.

'If you say so.'

'Oh, I do. Now, your father tells me that you are handling the personnel side of the business at present. Is that right?'

'Yes, why?'

'I shall probably want to change your duties later, when I've had time to see where your talents lie.'

He paused to watch for her reaction before continuing.

'But in that capacity, I want you to make up the salary of this member of staff now. He will be leaving within the hour.'

He handed a file to Nicky and she read the name on it.

'This is Gerald's file.' She looked up at him, puzzled. 'But why? He's been here for years.'

'I don't care if he's been here since

civilisation began. He's no good at his job and has to go. I realise this will probably put an enormous strain on your love life, but I'm sure you two will be able to sort out something.'

Nicky rose to her feet, shocked.

'But that's not fair. You can't come in here and, within minutes, start throwing people out!'

'I can and I have. Your father had agreed. Just do it, please.' He stood over her. 'Trust me, Nicky,' he said, as he left the office.

'Trust you? I'd sooner trust a tarantula,' she muttered at the closed door.

How could anyone feel safe in their job if, the minute he arrived, he started sacking the staff. Distraught, Nicky went straight to Gerald's office, but it was empty.

She had to get to the bottom of this. Jack couldn't be getting rid of Gerald because of her, could he? When Jack had carried her back from the beach, Gerald had made a fool of himself, telling Jack they were engaged, and obviously Jack still thought they were, even though she had tried to tell him at the time they weren't, but that was hardly a sacking matter. No, Jack wasn't petty. It must be something serious, but what?

The receptionist on duty told her Gerald had gone over to his house. Nicky bit her lip. She didn't particularly relish the idea of going to his home, but she had to see him.

What must he be thinking, Nicky wondered

43

as she left the hotel and started walking rapidly up the sandy drive towards Gerald's house. She had to tell him that it hadn't been hers or her father's idea.

The manager's house was on the edge of the estate, set amongst mahogany trees and quite private. The house had jalousied windows and wide verandas, but always gave Nicky the impression of being closed-up and secretive.

She often wondered if it was because Gerald was single, and spent more of his off-duty time in the hotel than he did at the house, that it had a shuttered look about it. She shrugged, remembering Gerald's disgust at her repeated refusals to visit him there.

His car was standing in the shade of the trees. As she approached, Nicky could see that its doors were open and boxes were stacked up nearby, ready to be loaded.

The sounds of activity reached her as she stepped on to the veranda and knocked at the open door. There was no reply so she walked through the door.

The room was in chaos. Packing cases were piled high, paintings stood against chairs and there was paper everywhere. Gerald was on his hands and knees in front of a large box, wrapping items in paper before stowing them away in the box.

Nicky cleared her throat.

'Hello, Gerald.'

He stopped what he was doing and looked

44

at her.

'Oh, it's you. Come to gloat, have you?'

'Why ever would I do that?'

She sat on the edge of the nearest chair and twisted her fingers together. This was going to be a lot harder than she had imagined.

'I've come to say how sorry I am to hear about you leaving.'

'I bet you are,' he replied sarcastically, getting to his feet and coming to stand near her.

'I don't understand. Why are you leaving? What happened?'

'That's good, coming from you. Playing Little Miss Innocence this morning, are you? Pretending you haven't got a clue about why I've been given the push?'

He moved closer and stood over her. Nicky frowned up at him.

'Of course, I don't know. That's why I'm here. Neither my father nor I knew about this.'

Angry splashes of colour stained his face and Nicky felt the first stirrings of fear. She was beginning to wonder if her decision to come here had been a wise one. He seemed to read her mind and threw an arm out to encompass the room.

'You've finally decided to grace this place with your presence,' he said, laughing bitterly. 'After all the times I've asked you here, you only manage it on the day I leave.'

Nicky couldn't hold his gaze.

'Listen, Gerald . . .'

'No! You listen! You're the reason I'm getting chucked out on my ear. Your lover obviously sees me as competition and wants to get rid of me so that he will have a clear field. What other reason could there be?'

Disturbed at what she was hearing, Nicky knew that no amount of talking would deter him from his ideas, but she had to try.

'If you mean Jack, he is not my lover, and I . . .'

'Oh, really? Tell that to the marines! The first time I saw him, you were wrapped around him making a spectacle of yourself. Don't forget, you even had to admit, in the end, that he was a stranger. You seriously expect me to believe that you aren't involved? You must think I'm stupid.'

Nicky blushed with embarrassment. How many other people thought the same thing, she wondered. Admittedly, Gerald was the only one who had been in the hotel hall that morning, but plenty of people had seen Jack carrying her across the beach, and what rumours had Gerald spread around in the meantime?

'No answer? I thought not,' he drawled. 'I think it's time I had a share of your attention. I've been around longer than he has, after all.'

Nicky's eyes opened in shock as she registered what he meant. She had to get away. She jumped to her feet in panic and tried to head for the door but he grabbed her arms.

'Going somewhere? I don't think so.' He pulled her closer. 'Let's see what happens when the Ice Maiden melts, shall we?'

Horror-stricken at the change that had come over him, Nicky couldn't believe this was the quiet, polite man she had known and worked with for so long. She tried to find excuses for his behaviour, but fear was sending icy fingers through her body and freezing her mind.

She twisted her head, hoping to avoid him as he crushed his mouth to hers. Just as Nicky reached screaming point, Jack's steely voice cut across the room.

'I think that's enough, don't you?'

His voice galvanised Gerald into action. He let Nicky go, almost throwing her from him and she wiped the back of her hand across her mouth in an effort to rid herself of Gerald's contaminating touch. Badly shaken, she hung on to a chair. She had no idea why Jack was here, but she had never been so glad to see anyone in her life. His glance was contemptuous as he jerked his head in the direction of the door.

'Go and wait for me in the Jeep,' he ordered.

'But, Jack . . .'

'Do as I say,' he commanded, his voice rising.

Nicky moved on unsteady legs towards the

door. Inside the house the tension reminded her of the silence before the arrival of a tropical storm. Outside, she was amazed to find the sun shining and the normal sounds of the day washed over her like a balm. She spotted the open-topped mini-moke that Jack used, askew in the drive, and she slumped gratefully into the passenger seat.

Seconds ticked by. Eventually, she heard Jack slam out of the house and walk over to the vehicle. He jumped into the driver's seat, slammed the door, revved the engine and accelerated wildly down the drive, leaving Nicky no option but to hang on if she was to avoid being thrown around.

She looked at him out of the corner of her eye as they bucked over the sleeping policemen. Jack's face was grim, his mouth tight-lipped, eyes angry and hostile. She grimaced. Silence was obviously the order of the day, she concluded, as they hurtled down the track towards the hotel.

Without warning, he wrenched the steering-wheel around. The tyres leaped across the track on to the manicured lawns and he headed the vehicle straight towards a stand of banyan trees.

Thick undergrowth had been allowed to cover the beard-like hanging roots and just as it seemed impossible that they would stop without crashing, the undergrowth gave way and the vehicle plunged into the middle of the trees, its undercarriage scraping against unresisting branches and foliage. A small flock of sugar birds rose into the air chattering in disgust as Jack hit the brakes and killed the engine.

Silence washed over them. Nicky looked upwards as she sagged against her seat. The monstrous trees had spread their thick, tangled roots to form a green canopy over them and the undergrowth screened them from the outside world.

Before she could drag in her first shaky breath of recovery, Jack said, 'I think you've got some explaining to do. I heard and saw enough up there to realise that you two couldn't possibly be engaged. Why did you lead me to believe that you were?'

'I never said we were, if you remember! That was Gerald's idea, not mine.'

'Then what on earth did you think you were doing, going up there on your own? Don't you know anything about men?'

She looked at him dazedly.

'I only went up to . . .'

He interrupted impatiently. 'Don't you know how he felt about you? Hadn't you any idea of the trouble you would be getting into? He was just like a smouldering fire and you went in offering a fan for the flames.'

For once, she was at a loss for words. She truly had no idea that Gerald felt like that about her, ignoring him outside their working relationship because he just didn't interest her emotionally. Many things became painfully clear to her, as Jack continued.

'I didn't see any signs of you kicking and screaming at him, so I presume his advances were acceptable, eh?'

Dismayed that he could put that interpretation on her actions she exclaimed, 'Jack, how could you even think that I . . . '

'What were you looking for?' he demanded. 'Excitement? Danger?'

'Excitement?' Nicky squeaked, her nerves almost in tatters.

If that was excitement she could quite happily live for the rest of her life without it!

'If you want to live dangerously, I'll give you danger,' he promised, his voice low and powerful.

Nicky looked at him. Her eyes were on a level with his mouth and she watched the sensual lips slowly forming his next words.

'And if it's excitement you want, you don't need to look any further than me.' She could only stare at him, unable to speak. 'Do you understand what I'm saying?' Nicky, who was now hopelessly confused, nodded anyway, then shook her head.

CHAPTER FIVE

From the day Jack came into her life, Nicky had been tossed about on the choppy seas of emotion, one minute on a crest, the next in a trough, yet nothing had prepared her for the feelings she had now.

She knew this was his way of punishing her for going to Gerald's on her own, but she didn't care. Just as long as he was near her, holding her.

Taking her head in his hands he kissed her passionately.

'I take it this will make things crystal clear?'

'Y-yes,' Nicky croaked, wondering if she would ever come down to earth again.

When she had recovered sufficiently, she thanked him for rescuing her and added, 'How did you know I was there?'

He laid an arm along the back of his seat and, catching a handful of her hair, wrapped strands of it around his fingers.

'Luckily I saw you heading up the track and asked one of the staff where it led. It seemed a good idea to take a look. But it was pure luck that I spotted you. Goodness knows what might have happened otherwise.'

Nicky shuddered at the thought.

'Just for the record, what exactly were you doing at Gerald's place?'

'I suppose I just wanted to find out why he had to leave.'

'You only had to ask me, Nicky. I would have told you. Do you remember the couple who stayed here last week?'

He named a particularly difficult pair of guests who had seemed to find fault with everything at the hotel.

'Yes, but how do you know about them?' she asked. 'They left on Tuesday.'

He nodded.

'They are friends of mine. They live on a neighbouring island. I paid for their visit and asked them to put the hotel through its paces to find out just how the staff coped with difficult guests.'

'What a terrible thing to do, spying on staff without them knowing,' Nicky snapped, irate at his underhand method.

'Not really. Think about it, Nicky. The staff are always on their best behaviour when we are around. It's only natural. The time you find out what they are really like is when they are dealing with the most important people around—the guests.'

Nicky could see the sense of what he was saying.

'But what happened with Gerald?'

'He wasn't as polite as he should have been, and a couple of times, when he told them he would sort out a problem, they didn't hear any more about it. He was also spotted trying to chat up one of the single female guests.'

'But he knows that isn't allowed. My father would be furious if he knew.'

Jack agreed, then added, 'Plus, he didn't handle the staff well either. He blamed them for everything that went wrong.'

That sounded like Gerald, Nicky thought, annoyed. He always had liked to put the blame on other people and wriggle out of any responsibility.

'You're very thorough,' she said.

'You have to be these days. Word of mouth is the best form of advertising, as you know, and if all the staff from top management downwards are giving their best, the guests notice and appreciate it. After all, they are here to enjoy themselves and that's what we want them to do.'

He reached for her hand and, unexpectedly, raised it to his mouth and placed a gentle kiss on the palm.

'Enough lectures for one day. We must go, before someone sends out a search party.'

He started up the engine and reversed out of the undergrowth. Nicky looked in horror at the gouge marks on the lawn and the flattened undergrowth and tried to imagine what the gardeners would make of it all!

*   *   *

The next few days passed in a blur for Nicky.

She had never worked so hard in her life, setting up the new working systems that Jack had devised.

A new manager was installed and he and his family moved into the house vacated by Gerald. The hotel buzzed with activity and far from finding the staff despondent when they knew that her father was now in partnership with Jack, Nicky was amazed to discover that they were as enthusiastic as she was.

The hotel grapevine worked overtime and finally came up trumps, reporting that not only was Jack not married, he liked to play the field! He worked long hours at the hotel, but went back to his yacht every night. Sometimes, when Nicky was taking a late-night walk along the beach before going to bed, she would see a single light shining on the boat, indicating that he was still working, despite the lateness of the hour.

Exactly a week after Gerald had been dismissed, Nicky walked into her office and found a young girl sitting at her desk. Joseph, the new manager, was explaining something to her. No-one came into her office unless invited yet here was a young girl whom she had never seen before making herself comfy and looking as if she was planning to stay. What was going on, she wondered.

'Do you have a problem here, Joseph?' she enquired.

Joseph looked up and smiled at her.

'No, no problem, Miss Nicky. I am just starting to teach this young lady how to do your work.'

'My work? What do you mean?' Nicky exclaimed.

'Well, you know, Mister Jack said I was to train someone to take your place as you wouldn't be doing this work any more, so that is what I am doing.'

He saw Nicky's surprised expression and the smile left his face.

'He did tell you about it, didn't he?'

Her mind racing, Nicky pulled herself together rapidly. She may have been completely unaware of the situation herself, but she couldn't afford to let the staff know that.

'Of course he did, Joseph. I had forgotten it would be today.'

His smile returned.

'Oh, that's all right then. He told me to tell you that he would be upstairs with your father when you wanted to see him.'

'Thank you, Joseph. I'll do that now.'

She had difficulty forcing a smile, but did her best, hoping she didn't look as shocked as she felt, and praying that her legs would carry her out of the office.

Once outside, she shut the door and leaned against it, her eyes closed. Breathe deeply, she told herself, breathe deeply. This is just a bad dream.

No, it isn't, a little voice said in her head. He's finally got rid of you and hasn't even the guts to say so to your face!

I should have known what he was up to when he fired Gerald, she thought, furious with herself for being taken in by his slick words. It's quite obvious now that he plans to get rid of all the management staff and put in his own people.

Nicky was aware that her father had already signed the partnership contract. She frowned. She knew her father well enough to know that there would always be a position for her at the hotel while he was here, but what if Jack had outwitted him? Could he get away with it?

'If he thinks he's getting rid of me without a fight, he's got another thing coming,' she said under her breath.

She stoked her anger each step of the way up to her father's office.

'I'll kill him when I get my hands on him,' she muttered as she strode along the corridor.

When she reached the office door, she threw it open without knocking and went in. The two men had been chatting and enjoying a laugh when she appeared, her father leaning back in his chair, Jack sitting on the opposite side of the desk, ankles crossed and feet on its edge.

She stopped in the middle of the room, put her hands on her hips and glared at Jack.

'What do you mean by firing me?' she

stormed at him. 'You can't do that to me! I won't let you, and besides, I refuse to resign. So what do you plan to do about that?'

He put his head to one side and returned her gaze steadily, his eyes sparkling.

'She certainly looks wonderful when she's mad, don't you think, David?' he asked Nicky's father.

'Yes, I would have to agree with you there, Jack, although I don't know where she gets it from. It isn't from my side of the family, that's for sure, and certainly not from her mother's side either, come to think of it.'

'A throw-back then, would you say, David?'

'Mmm, yes, very probably,' her father said, trying hard not to laugh.

Nicky stamped a foot on the carpet.

'Will you two stop talking about me as if I was a piece of flotsam that just washed up on the beach. I've just come from my office where Joseph is teaching someone to do my work and I demand . . .'

'Oh-oh,' her father said getting to his feet. 'I think I'll leave you two young people together now. I'll be late for my appointment in Bridgetown.'

'Pops, do you mean that you knew about this and didn't tell me?'

'Pick on someone your own size, Nicky, and let your father get off for his appointment,' Jack interrupted.

David said his goodbyes and left the office

chuckling to himself.

'Right, let's get to the bottom of this,' Nicky said, rounding on Jack.

'I think that's a good idea,' he replied, grabbing her by the arm and dragging her across to the desk.

'Let me go,' she spat out, frantically trying to escape him.

'No,' came the reply as he leaned back against the desk, legs astride, and pulled her to him. He grabbed her arms and pinned them behind her back.

'Now, fire away,' he invited. 'Get it off your chest.'

'Don't think you are going to come out of this smelling of roses, Jack Morgan, because you aren't!' she burst out, determined to fire the first shot.

His face was serious.

'Of course not. I wouldn't dream of it,' he said, shaking his head.

'There is someone in my office, a complete stranger.'

'Yes.'

'You arranged this?'

'Yes.'

'Stop saying yes.'

'OK.'

'You didn't tell me. Why am I surrounded by men who don't tell me things?'

'I did tell you.'

'No, you didn't.'

'Yes, I did.'

She felt his hands moving up her back. He reached her neck and slowly massaged each joint. She closed her eyes and leaned her head back into his hands as he lowered his mouth to place a whisper of a kiss on her throat.

'Jack . . .'

'Yes?'

'Jack, don't do that.' She struggled feebly in his grasp.

'But you like it,' he said, nuzzling her neck.

'I know, but stop it.'

'Whatever you say.'

He raised his head and smiled down at her, his eyes warm as summer seas and Nicky wondered how she had ever thought them cold. The sharp edges were being knocked off her anger, but it was hard to focus on anything. She forced herself to make one last effort to get some sort of answer from Jack.

'When did you tell me, Jack?' she whispered.

'Do you remember when you were photocopying all those packs for the drugs company convention staying here next week?'

They were making some headway at last. She could remember the day as if it had been yesterday. Come to think of it, it had been yesterday!

'You still with me?' Jack continued.

'Yes.'

He moved his mouth around to her ear and

whispered, fanning warm air in her ear and down the side of her neck. She shivered deliciously.

'Well, as I remember it—correct me if I'm wrong—you had piles of paper everywhere, on the floor, all over your desk, and the photocopier was making a lot of noise, so you didn't hear me come in.'

His low whispering had an intimate quality to it which drove Nicky almost to the brink of distraction.

'Then I tiptoed up behind you . . .'

She squeezed her eyes tight shut and groaned, only too aware of what he had done after that.

'Don't you remind me!'

'Oh . . . OK . . . so I said to you I thought your talents were being wasted, that someone else could do photocopying and the like, and we should get someone in to do it for you. That would leave you free to concentrate on the overseeing of the new projects we are planning, and invent new ways to keep the guests happy.'

Nicky frowned.

'I vaguely remember you saying something like that yesterday.'

'Good. For a minute there, I thought we weren't getting anywhere.'

She opened one eye and, leaning back, peered up at him. He looked straight back, his expression giving nothing away.

'I only did what we discussed and agreed on, Nicky,' he said, planting a kiss on the end of her nose.

'But I thought you meant sometime in the future.'

'So I did. Today is sometime in the future. It's a whole twenty-four hours in the future.'

'You're a fast mover.'

'If you mean that I don't hang around when I've made up my mind, I would have to agree. Anyway, enough of work. We've both been working hard lately. Let's take the rest of the day off and go for a picnic.'

His suggestion threw her, and she felt her anger deflate.

'A picnic?'

'Yes. Why not? It would be a good idea to investigate this suggestion of yours to organise tours from the hotel for the guests, instead of having them make their own arrangements.'

'Really?'

'I've got a copy here of every leaflet we have in reception on tourist attractions. Let's look through them and see if we can come up with a few ideas.'

They sat at the desk pouring over the literature, discussing suitable places to visit and eventually agreed on a tour which included several of the island's famous attractions and which they thought could be comfortably tackled by their guests in a day.

'Right,' Jack said, gathering up the leaflets

they intended to take with them. 'Let's meet in the carpark in half an hour. The last one there pays the forfeit!'

'And just what would that be?' Nicky asked warily.

'Who knows? The winner gets to choose,' Jack said, already on his way out of the office.

Nicky ran after him. If there was a winner, it followed that there must also be a loser, and she wanted to make certain that it wasn't her.

CHAPTER SIX

Nicky wasted precious minutes deciding on a suitable outfit. She eventually chose a silk, short-sleeved T-shirt in coral pink and a skirt in the same shade with cream stripes.

She brushed her hair out of its single plait and allowed it to fall in waves down her back, holding it back on each side of her face with tortoise-shell combs.

Giving her face only a cursory glance, she pushed her feet into strappy sandals and, picking up her bag, she checked the time on her watch. Good, just twenty minutes since they had parted. She was going to be well within the time limit and, with luck, would be the first to arrive.

She left her cottage at a fast walk, excited at the prospect of a whole day in Jack's company and determined not to be caught out and lose the bet in the last few minutes. But as she came in sight of the carpark, she stopped in amazement. Sitting in his Jeep and looking as if he had been waiting for her for hours was Jack!

Her shoulders slumped dejectedly as she made her way slowly across to the vehicle. How could he possibly have got here so soon, she wondered.

He had changed into a short-sleeved shirt which set off his eyes to perfection and a pair of white slacks. On the rear seat was a picnic hamper and a cold-box.

'What kept you?' he asked, tossing the newspaper he had been reading on to the floor at the rear.

She regarded him mutinously as she settled into the passenger seat and, without preamble, asked, 'How did you manage it? You must have cheated.'

He smiled at her smugly.

'Not at all. Just good management and forward planning.'

Nicky, who had spent most of the time whilst getting ready contemplating what exquisite forms of torture his forfeit would consist of, was piqued to find him here ahead of her.

'Do you always set out to win?'

Her looked at her seriously.

'Only if the prize is worth winning,' he

answered.

She turned away, afraid he would see how bitterly disappointed she was. He started the engine and put the car into gear.

Away from the hotel, they turned north on to Highway One, skirting the white, curving beaches set against the dazzling Caribbean.

On such a beautiful day, it was impossible for Nicky to stay mad at him for long. The temperature was in the lower eighties and the sweet scent of frangipani trees wafted around them, blown by the gentle winds.

'We'll stick to our plan and go to St Peter first, yes?' Jack asked.

'OK.'

They travelled in companionable silence, Nicky marvelling at the ease with which Jack could change from dynamic businessman to sun-loving tourist, seemingly at the drop of a hat.

They spent some time walking around the Bajan fishing village before finding a cool spot to stop and drink large glasses of cold fruit juice. Jack was fascinated by the traditional wooden shops and houses, and Nicky began to see through fresh eyes.

'Have you been here before?' she asked.

'Not here,' he replied. 'My only recollections of Barbados were when my parents brought me to the island as a young boy, so this is all a new experience for me. This village is refreshing, though. There's so much sophistication on this coast that a stop here will be a real change for the guests.'

They then headed inland, their progress slowed somewhat by the donkey carts which frequented the local roads. They passed chattel houses painted in shades of chocolate, coffee and banana-yellow, some of their gardens with sheets and pillowcases spread over lawns to bleach in the sun.

The remainder of the morning was spent wandering around a three-hundred-year-old property owned by the Barbados National Trust. It was still one of the centres for sugar cane production on the island and, as such, they both felt it to be an ideal location for guests to visit.

The interior of the house was resplendent with antiques and beautiful furniture made from the local mahogany trees. Jack seemed to find it necessary to remain close to Nicky's side as they wandered from room to room, brushing his bare arm against hers when pointing out something he thought she should see and breathing warmly on her neck as he leaned over to whisper snippets of information from the guide book to her.

By the time their tour was at an end, Nicky was sensitised almost beyond endurance and hurried out of the building to the heat of the day, forcing herself to put some distance between them, afraid of her feelings and her lack of control over them.

They found a place to stop for a late lunch, above a little resort town of Bathsheba perched on the cliffs of the east coast. Laying a rug on the ground, they unpacked the hamper and cool-box to the accompaniment of the wild Atlantic breakers as they crashed on to the coral shore below.

They talked as they ate, Nicky relaxing enough to enjoy the conversation and ask questions of her own.

'What made you decide on owning hotels as a career? Did your parents have one?'

He swallowed some wine before answering.

'No. My father had taken over the family's nutmeg estate from my grandfather and hoped that I would follow him when I was old enough, but he lost everything when it was hit by a hurricane, and had to look around for something else to do.'

'Couldn't he have planted more, if he was so keen to have you in the business?'

'He simply didn't have enough money or time to wait. The hurricane devastated the estate and it needed total replanting. Replacement trees take nine years to crop, so he would have had to let most of the staff go and hope some of them would still be available for work when the new crop was ready.

'Besides, although I was only nineteen, I had made it pretty obvious that nutmeg growing wasn't for me. I had been reading my grandfather's financial papers since I was knee-high to a grasshopper and when he saw that I had an eye for it and could pick my own investments, he used to give me money or buy me shares for my birthdays and Christmas.

'Before long, I was using the money to buy my own, and when he died, he left me a large sum of money which I invested.'

'And the hotels?'

'A fluke, really. I lent quite a substantial amount of money to a friend who couldn't pay it back. It happened around the time we lost the nutmeg, and it seemed like two disasters at once, but the friend wanted to leave the islands and gave me a run-down hotel he owned as payment for the debt.'

Jack wrapped his arms around his knees and stared out over the water below.

'My parents decided to put what money they had into it and we muddled through, making one mistake after another, learning as we went.'

He laughed. 'And we made a few, I can tell you. As time went on, I realised I quite enjoyed the challenge, and my parents were happy, so we kept it.'

'Do they still run it now?'

'No. My father died in a boating accident when I was twenty-one and my mother died of a heart attack eight months later.'

Nicky, who had lost her own mother when she was fourteen, felt his pain. There were no words she could say to him that could be of comfort, so she reached across to take his hand and squeezed it. He glanced at her, smiled, and squeezed back.

'Thank you,' he said quietly.

'You were very young to have coped with all that,' she continued.

'Responsibility makes you grow up quickly, Nicky,' he commented, 'but I was lucky. I had Mike. He turned up at the estate one day looking for work, and just stayed. When we moved to the hotel, he came with us.'

Nicky remembered the big American who had been so kind to her on Jack's yacht when she had her accident.

'Now he skippers the yacht for me and makes sure I get where I have to go on time, besides doing a hundred other small things to oil the wheels on my life. He's looked out for me for so long he can't seem to break the habit, I guess. He tells me that if I'm thinking of getting rid of him, forget it! He's here to stay.'

'But don't you have any other family?' Nicky asked as she opened a flask of coffee and poured some for them both.

'Yes, I've a sister, but she is a few years older than me and was already married and living abroad.'

'Do you see her very often?'

He gave her a guarded look.

'No, not much.'

Nicky lay back on the rug and looked up at

the clear, azure sky. She understood now why her father had been so intent on selling the hotel. He knew that if he died suddenly, she would have no relatives to help out, and he might have left her with debts which she couldn't meet if Jack hadn't been prepared to buy the hotel.

Jack leaned back on the rug and, propping himself up on one elbow, said, 'A penny for them.'

She smiled. 'I was just thinking about Pops. He's absolutely delighted that you decided to be his partner instead of buying him out direct, you know. He never said, but I think he had been worrying about leaving me with problems if he died suddenly. We'll always be grateful to you, Jack.'

'I'm not looking for gratitude, Nicky. Although I've never had a partnership before, I don't see why it shouldn't work.'

'Wasn't it a bit unusual, though, when you hadn't even signed a contract, to give us so much money so soon?'

There, she had asked him at last. He didn't meet her eyes when answering.

'Not really. I trusted your father and he was desperately in need of working capital. Simple as that.'

His reason didn't ring true to Nicky even now, but she knew it would be pointless to push Jack for any further revelations. He would just clam up.

'The hotel has been my father's life since my mother died. He wants to do what is best for it,' she maintained. 'He puts all his energy into his work.'

'Yes, I know. That's why I wanted you to give up the things you are doing now and do more for your father. He needs to ease up. There's no reason to think he may ever have another heart attack, but if we relieve the pressure for him, it will lessen his chances.'

No matter what he says, Nicky thought, Jack is a very caring man and I will always be thankful that he was the person my father approached first.

'But why the necessity for such speed?' she questioned. 'We agreed the idea yesterday and already someone has taken over my work.'

'Nicky, I just don't have time to wait. I've got three hotels and a whole package of investments, none of which runs itself.'

He ran a hand through his thick hair.

'It would be wonderful to be able to stay at your hotel for months on end and gradually get things right, but I need to get all the new systems in place and the hiccups ironed out before I leave.'

'What do you mean, leave?'

A cold hand of fear gripped Nicky's heart. Leave? What was he talking about? He had only just arrived, hadn't he?

'I can't always be based at the hotel, you know.'

'But you live on the yacht, not in the hotel. I thought you said you used the yacht as your base.'

He smiled at her.

'And I do, but even though I have good managers, I have to visit my other hotels regularly. I can't stay anchored out in your bay indefinitely. You understand that, don't you, Nicky?'

No, I don't, she wanted to shout at him. I don't understand anything any more. Why you have to go, why you can't stay. Why one day I don't want you around and the next I can't seem to live without you.

Her voice shook as she asked, 'Will you just vanish into thin air?'

'Of course not. I'll be around until I'm satisfied that everything is running well and then I shall be popping back from time to time.'

Nicky got to her knees abruptly and began tidying up, crashing plates together and throwing glasses and knives haphazardly into the hamper.

'Popping back from to time? That's good of you! I'm amazed you trust Pops and me to look after the place in your absence.'

Her voice was cold as steel. Jack sat up and grabbed her arm, effectively stopping her from wrecking any more crockery.

'What exactly do you mean by that?' he asked, surprised.

'You . . . you walk into people's lives, turn them upside down and then walk calmly out again without a backward glance.'

She felt hot tears begin to gather behind her eyes, and looked away. Unable to keep them in check, they started falling down her cheeks in earnest. Jack watched them and a smile suddenly lit up his face.

'My sister always says that a woman only cries if she is pregnant—or in love. Which are you, Nicky?'

He ran his hands comfortingly up and down her bare arms.

'Oh, shut up, Jack Morgan. I'm neither, and never have been. How dare you even suggest otherwise. Let me go,' she retorted, trying to break free of his grip.

'I don't think so, not until you've answered some questions.' He grabbed her chin and forced her around to face him. 'You'll miss me?'

She knocked his hand away angrily.

'Miss you? Who would miss you? You're nothing but trouble. Nobody would miss you, and certainly not me.'

'Don't you think that was rather over the top for someone who professes to dislike me?'

Too late, she saw the light of battle in his eyes. He held her gaze for what seemed like an eternity and then said quietly, 'Let's put that to the test, shall we?'

Puzzled, Nicky said, 'What do you mean?'

A slow, lazy smile crossed his face and Nicky suddenly knew what he meant.

'Let's say that this is your forfeit for being late this morning. We'll find out what you really feel for me, shall we?'

Nicky was horrified at his suggestion. Already struggling to keep control of her feelings for him, she knew it would be impossible to hide them from him if he was determined to find out. She started to shake her head.

'Oh, no, Jack, no.'

He gently pushed her back on the rug and lowered his head to hers. His kisses were torture to her. Unable to resist, she gave herself up wholeheartedly to them, winding her fingers in his hair and pulling him closer to her. Returning his kisses, matching fire with fire, time stood still for her.

Nicky was unable to hide her feelings for him, but she told herself that, if he walked out of her life tomorrow, she would always have the memory of this one, perfect day. And perhaps, with luck, he might not realise how she felt about him.

Much later, Jack propped himself up on one elbow and smiled down at her.

'You're beautiful, Nicky, truly beautiful.'

And as Nicky gradually became aware of the sounds of the day, the pounding of the waves on the shore below, the soft hum of the whistling frogs, she knew, without a shadow of doubt, that she had fallen in love.

CHAPTER SEVEN

They drove south to Gun Hill and watched the monkeys swinging through the trees, then stood at the top of the hill surveying the view for miles around.

Later, as it grew dark, they dropped down into Bridgetown and wandered around the streets admiring the high-masted schooners moored in the Careenage and the windows of the stores in Broad Street, before ending up at Baxter's Road as they considered the wares of the 'cutter' shops, as the locals called the small sandwich bars. It was Friday, and the old women were frying fish over braziers in the open air. Nicky sniffed the air appreciatively.

'I'm starving,' Nicky said after a while.

'Come on then, let's find a restaurant and get you something to eat,' Jack replied, grasping her hand and pulling her along.

'No, Jack,' she said, tugging him back. 'I'd much prefer some flying fish, right here, from one of those stalls in the open.'

He looked at her closely.

'OK, whatever you say.'

She smiled. 'And perhaps a bottle of cold beer?'

They ate their fish in silence as they walked

slowly, gazing in the shop windows. Afterwards, they drove back to the hotel in companionable silence.

When Jack escorted her to her cottage suite, she asked him in for a nightcap, but he wouldn't hear of it.

'You need your beauty sleep and I've work to do.' He kissed her. 'Sweet dreams, darling girl,' he said and walked away into the night.

Nicky was hardly aware of going through her nightly beauty routine before climbing into bed, and was asleep in minutes.

*　　　*　　　*

Jack's yacht was not anchored in the bay when Nicky took her early-morning swim, and disappointment trickled through her. It was true, she acknowledged to herself, that he didn't have to account to her for every minute of his day, but surely, after yesterday, they had come some way to being closer?

Nicky spent hours watching the horizon when she should have been working, so she saw the yacht motor slowly into sight on the morning of the third day and anchor in the bay. She spent the day floating on air, all concentration gone, the thought of seeing Jack again uppermost in her mind.

As the hours passed and Jack still had not made an appearance at the hotel, her feelings of elation slowly vanished to be replaced by indignation.

She tried to tell herself that she was angry with him for being so irresponsible as to neglect the hotel, but she knew that was a lie. She felt hurt that Jack had been back for most of the day and hadn't come to see her, as though she meant nothing to him.

A frown wrinkling her brow, she paced her office, hands thrust deep into her pockets, thinking. It would be wonderful to see him, and soon, but would she have to wait for him to come to her?

Suddenly, she stopped pacing. She had an idea. There were some papers requiring Jack's signature. She would take them out to the yacht and see him, right now. Grabbing them from her desk, she stuffed them into a file and left the office at a run.

It was a flimsy excuse, she knew. The papers weren't needed for another week, but it was the best she could come up with at short notice.

Within minutes, Nicky had taken the hotel's small dinghy and gone across to the yacht, knotting a rope securely to the bathing ladder and climbing aboard. There were no signs of life, although the doors to the saloon were open. She knocked on the glass door and shouted.

'Hello, anyone on board?'

She could hear the faint sound of music, and some mouth-watering smells were coming from the general direction of the galley. A grey-haired head appeared from below, followed by a body. It was Mike. He walked towards her through the dining area and down the few steps to the main saloon.

'Well, if it isn't the little lady,' he said, extending his hand and beaming at her. 'Hi. How are you feeling now?'

'I'm fine, Mike, thanks,' she replied.

'Good, good. Well, what can I do for you?'

'It's Jack I've come to see,' Nicky said, sitting down on the off-white leather settee.

She threw the file on to a nearby table.

'He's not here, I'm sorry to say.'

'Oh, well, will it be OK if I wait for him?'

Mike looked flustered. He seemed embarrassed at her arrival and Nicky was contrite. It had been a silly thing to do, to come out here on the spur of the moment and it looked like Mike was having trouble knowing what to say to her. Perhaps Jack didn't like visitors on board when he wasn't around, and Mike didn't know how to tell her.

'I'm sorry,' she said, standing up again. 'That was very rude of me. The smells are lovely. I should have realised you're busy cooking. You won't want me hanging around.'

'Oh, no, not really,' he said, suddenly noticing the single, cut-crystal glass on the table. 'I was just having a cool drink.'

He picked it up and Nicky's eyes caught sight of the lipstick on the rim of the glass.

She looked at him, puzzled, then a female voice broke the silence.

'We've got a visitor! How lovely. I couldn't hear anything over the sound of the radio. Why didn't you tell me, Mike?'

They both turned to look at the woman descending the steps to the saloon. She had an apron covering her shorts and top and was wiping her hands on a tea-cloth.

'Well, I . . . um.'

Mike lifted the hand that wasn't holding the glass and let it fall to his side. The new arrival shook her head and smiled.

'He's hopeless,' she said, taking off her apron and throwing it, together with the tea-cloth, on to the table.

Nicky stared at her. She was the most gorgeous creature she had ever seen, small and petite with blonde curls that tumbled down on to her shoulders, big brown eyes and a bone structure Nicky would have died for. She judged her to be about ten years older than herself, but it was hard to say. She had the timeless elegance only money could buy.

She was also, as Nicky could plainly see, in the early stages of pregnancy. The older woman walked over to Nicky, smiling, and held out her hand.

'It's obviously no good waiting for Mike to do the honours. He'll be here all day. I'm Emerald, and you are?'

'Nicky—Nicky Kington,' she said, startled.

78

'Jack's friend from the hotel?' Emerald asked.

Nicky nodded. Jack had obviously been talking about her to this woman, but who was she? Suddenly Nicky remembered Jack talking to Mike about an Emerald the day she had her accident and had been brought to the yacht. What was it they had said about her? She couldn't remember.

'How lovely,' Emerald was saying. 'Come and sit down, so we can get to know one another. It's always nice to meet a friend of Jack's.'

She moved across to the settee and sat down gracefully, making Nicky feel like an oversized, clumsy whale.

'I mustn't stop. I only came out to—'

'Come on, Nicky,' she said, patting the settee. 'I want to know all about you.'

At her words, Mike made an inarticulate sound in his throat and looked uncomfortable. Emerald looked up at him.

'For goodness' sake, Mike, go and polish some brasses, or whatever you do best. And don't run off with my drink,' she said, holding out her hand. 'You can see I haven't finished with it yet.'

Nicky glanced at Mike who had the grace to look embarrassed. She had the oddest feeling he hadn't wanted the two women to meet, but why? Unseen currents were drifting on the air around her, she felt certain.

The older woman propped herself up with cushions at her back and when Mike pushed a stool towards the settee, she obediently raised her legs and rested them on it.

'You know Jack says you are supposed to be resting,' he said sternly.

'I know that,' Emerald said, glancing at Nicky. 'If he had his way,' she said, gesturing with her head towards Mike, 'I'd be in my cabin stretched out, and preferably asleep, all day, every day. But while he's here, let him get you a drink. A glass of champagne, perhaps? I adore it, but am not allowed to drink it now,' she said, smiling smugly and patting her tummy. 'And I miss it, so I'm always trying to force it on my friends.'

'No . . . no, thanks. I really have to be getting back, you know.'

'Oh, not yet, surely. You've only just arrived.'

She waved a hand at Mike, who was still hovering, and shooed him away.

'Do you have any brothers, Nicky?' she asked.

'No, I don't.'

Emerald grimaced.

'Well, don't have any, if you want my advice. They can be a terrible nuisance.'

Nicky smiled at her, feeling drawn to Emerald in spite of her unease at being here. So this must be Mike's sister.

'Jack is thrilled about the baby, you know,'

80

she continued. 'He says it took me so long to get this way that I have to look after myself, especially now I'm so old! The cheeky devil!' She laughed. 'The only trouble is that he and Mike fuss over me so much I feel like I'm being suffocated.'

Nicky froze as the implications of what she was hearing began to sink in. No wonder Mike didn't want us to meet, she thought unhappily. It must be Jack's baby she's having. What other interpretation could she put on what she had just heard?

She's pregnant and they aren't even married, for hadn't the hotel grapevine told her that? Morals certainly weren't as high as they used to be, she acknowledged, but she never thought that Jack would have behaved this way.

The desire to check for signs of a wedding ring was overpowering and her eyes were drawn irresistibly to the other woman's hand. What she saw made her even more mystified.

Every single finger and thumb had rings on them, sometimes two or three on each finger. There were diamonds, opals, sapphires and, of course, emeralds but, as far as Nicky could see, no wedding ring.

Emerald saw her look and laughed.

'Awful, isn't it?' she said, displaying her hands for Nicky to have a better look. 'We were burgled once, you know, and I lost all my jewels. The insurance company paid out, of course, but it's not the same, is it?' she declared, naturally assuming that Nicky would know what it was like to own vast amounts of expensive jewellery.

'Some of my rings had great sentimental value. Now if I can't wear them all at once, I don't buy them. That way, if we are burgled again, the thieves won't get my jewellery. Luckily, my tastes never ran to earrings, or I dread to think what I would look like now.'

Nicky forced a tight smile but her senses were reeling, and she wished she had never been so impulsive and come to the yacht. Desperate to get away and be on her own to come to terms with what she now knew, she stood up.

'I'm sorry, I really do have to go.'

Emerald's face fell.

'Oh, do stay. Jack will be back any minute, and I've made a fish casserole for supper. It's his favourite. Do stay and eat with us. I'm sure he'd like that.'

I don't think so, Nicky thought. In fact, when he knows that I am aware of what is going on, he will probably be furious to discover that I have been here at all.

'Perhaps you would give him the file when he comes back?' she said, walking backwards towards the glass doors as she spoke. 'Say goodbye to Mike for me, please.'

She didn't stop for an answer, just kept walking across the aft deck and hurried down the bathing ladder to her dinghy.

The sound of an outboard engine floated across to her on the evening breeze and she turned around uneasily, to see the yacht's dinghy coming across the bay, Jack at the tiller.

Nicky felt her heart sink. How was she to escape him now? In a frantic attempt to get away before he reached the yacht, she started the engine and fumbled with the rope's knot. In her haste, her fingers refused to co-operate. He pulled alongside.

'This is a surprise. To what do I owe this pleasure?' he asked.

'I . . . I just . . . well . . . I just brought some papers for you to sign,' she managed to get out, tugging on the rope.

He frowned. 'Oh? What papers?'

If Nicky told him, she knew he would realise how unimportant her visit had been and want to know what had prompted it. At the moment, she didn't feel capable of thinking of anything which would satisfy his curiosity without giving away the truth. She couldn't stay and be humiliated. There was only one thing for it.

'Sorry, Jack, I can't hear you,' she shouted, finally managing to free the rope.

'Hang on a minute,' he said, putting out a hand to hold the side of her dinghy. 'I want to speak to you.'

But Nicky, quite frantic now with the need

to put as much distance between them as possible, had already put the outboard motor into reverse. Jack refused to let go as the dinghy moved away from the yacht, and was pulled into the water.

'Just what are you playing at?' he yelled, as he surfaced and slicked the water out of his eyes.

He hadn't secured his dinghy when he reached the yacht, too intent on talking to Nicky, and now it rose and fell on the wake of her tiny boat, moving away gently from the yacht.

As she turned her boat and headed for the shore, she watched him securing his dinghy and pulling himself out of the water.

Devastated when he had gone overboard, she wanted to stay to make sure that he was all right, but Mike and Emerald had come out on to the deck to see what the commotion was, and her need to get away was paramount.

She glanced back once more, to see Jack, wet but safe, climbing up the swimming ladder, then she opened the engine's throttle as if her life depended on it, racing for the shore as fast as she could.

Once she had tied up at the jetty, she didn't stop running until she was safely back in her cottage. She slammed the door, locking it securely, and leaned back against it, tears streaming down her face. Shock finally caught up with her and she started to shake.

'Jack, Jack,' she sobbed, 'how could you have done this to me?'

What sort of man could make a woman pregnant and then callously pretend to love another? Thank goodness she had found out. It was too late to save her heart, but at least she could salvage some pride.

It was obvious she would have to leave the hotel. Goodness knows what her father would have to say about it, but staying here and knowing she might run into Jack or Emerald at any time would be impossible.

Once, Nicky had imagined that she could cope with seeing Jack with someone else, but since she had tasted his kisses and felt his strong arms holding her, she knew how soul-destroying it would be. Better never to see him again than die slowly inside.

It was no-one's fault but hers. Hadn't she virtually thrown herself at him last week? A warm blush spread over her. What could he possibly have said to her? Excuse me, I want to kiss you, and I'd certainly like to get to know you better, but I must tell you before I do that I already have a girlfriend who is pregnant, and I'm not married to her.

He may have made all the running, but she knew in her heart of hearts that she had encouraged him, and the knowledge did not sit very well on her.

A thunderous knock on the door behind her had Nicky leaping away from it, a hand over her mouth.

'I know you're in there, Nicky, so open up.'

It was Jack! Nicky brushed the angry tears away with the knuckles of one hand, her heart pounding in her chest. The last thing she was about to do was to tell Jack she was inside. She could almost hear him listening. She waited. He banged on the door again.

'If you don't open up this door by the time I have counted to three, I'm going to break it down,' he raged at her. 'One, two . . .'

Nicky could well believe that he would do as he said. After all, he had proved himself to be a man of his word, but what would the guests who happened to pass by think? She dreaded to imagine.

'Three.'

He shouldered the door, and Nicky felt it give slightly. It wouldn't take him long to break it down at this rate. There was nothing for it but to open the door.

It creaked as she unlocked and then opened it and Jack pushed past her, closing and locking it again after him. He turned to face her, anger written on every feature.

He was wearing the same clothes he had on when she had seen him last, and was soaking wet. She wanted to laugh hysterically, but one look in his eyes was enough to kill the idea.

'Don't even think it,' he ground out. 'Start talking, but it had better be good, whatever your excuses.'

86

'I don't know what you mean,' she said primly.

He advanced slowly towards her.

'Don't take that line with me. I want answers, and I want them now.'

Her eyes were drawn to the way his chest rose and fell under the wet clothes. She bit down on a sob.

'Well? Why didn't you tell me you were coming out to the yacht? I could have saved you a journey.'

Nicky started to back away, frightened.

'I . . .' She cleared her throat. 'I brought out some papers for you to sign,' she managed to get out.

'I've seen them. They're unimportant. Papers that could have waited until next week.' He shook his head. 'You'll have to do better than that.'

There was no question of Nicky telling him the real reason she had been out there. She had humiliated herself enough for one day, without admitting that she had rushed to see him because she had missed him.

For all she knew, he would just laugh in her face.

'How were we to know that you would be around next week?' she gasped.

'Because I would have told you if I was going to be away.'

'Oh, really? Just like you told us this time?'

He gave an exasperated sigh, as though he

87

was trying hard to get through to a very dim person.

'I'm always just on the end of a phone, Nicky. I hadn't gone to the other end of the world. It would have been a simple thing to have called me if you needed anything.'

She drew herself up to her full height and stared up at him defiantly, refusing to see the sense of his statement.

'How you've got the nerve to come here and lecture me, when you've got a woman out there living with you, I don't know.'

'What are you talking about?'

'As if you didn't know. Emerald, of course.'

'Emerald?' He looked wary. 'What has she got to do with this?'

'Everything, I would have thought,' Nicky said, her chest heaving with fury. 'Not only is she pregnant, she's unmarried as well.'

'Emerald might be a lot of things, but unmarried is not one of them,' he retorted, his voice rising.

Nicky's mouth fell open and she nearly choked.

'She's married?' she spluttered.

'Most definitely.'

She tried to raise her hand to push hair out of her eyes, but Jack's grip held her captive.

'That's worse! She's married and pregnant and she's left her husband to live with you! How could you do it?'

'For goodness' sake, Nicky, you aren't

88

thinking straight!'

'That's right, put the blame on me now,' she interrupted.

'I was merely going to say that you are jumping to conclusions without knowing the facts. Emerald has not left her . . .'

He stopped speaking and stared at her, as if he had said too much.

'Go on then, deny it,' Nicky raged.

He didn't speak.

'You can't deny it because it's true, isn't it?'

He held her gaze steadily, searching her face.

'I've had to trust you, Nicky, and at some stage in your life you are going to have to trust me. After the day we spent together, I thought you had reached that point, but it seems I was wrong. If that's what you want to think, I can't stop you,' he said quietly, 'but if you honestly believe that I could do such a thing, there's nothing more to be said.'

Her rage running out of control, Nicky drew back her arm and slapped his face hard. In the small room it sounded like a pistol shot. An angry, red mark appeared on the side of his face as he stood looking at her. Then he turned around slowly, opened the door and walked away. She watched him go and then closed the door, leaning her back against it.

Mortified at her behaviour, she knew she had pushed him too far. Her legs finally refused to support her and, as she slid slowly down the door to the floor, she cried as though her heart was breaking.

CHAPTER EIGHT

After Jack left, Nicky lay awake all night, too exhausted even to do more than lie on the covers. Desolation crept over her and she was unable even to form coherent thoughts, let alone try to make sense of what had happened between them.

The early-morning light filtered through her bedroom shutters and she turned her head towards it disconsolately, all thought of her usual, morning swim forgotten.

The only thing she did know with any certainty was that she couldn't leave her father. She had seriously contemplated it on her dash back from the yacht the previous evening, but it hadn't really been an option.

She would have to give him some sort of explanation, and she knew he would be heartbroken to think that, by bringing in Jack to save the hotel, he had unwittingly caused Nicky so much pain.

No, there was only one course open to her. She would have to carry on as though nothing had happened. After all, she thought, as she dragged herself off the bed and headed for the bathroom, it was only the end of a love affair, wasn't it? Not much of an affair, either, when you thought about it—a few, chaste kisses. She blushed. Well, perhaps not so chaste, she amended hastily, remembering the passion which had flared between them.

Her head ached and her eyes were red and sore from lack of sleep as she turned the water on in the shower in an effort to banish last night's scene from her mind. But she had to admit defeat, and a tear escaped from under tightly-closed lids.

Outside, the sun sparkled and danced on the water and Nicky could hear the happy chatter and laughter of the guests as she passed the cottages on her way to the hotel. The rattle of crockery and the aroma of fresh coffee greeted her as she walked across the hotel's terrace, making her stomach turn over at the thought of having to eat anything. Out in the bay, the yacht rode silently at anchor, gleaming white, mocking her.

Apprehensive about meeting her father before she had managed to get her emotions under control, she made her way tentatively to the office she now shared with him. He was well-tuned to her feelings, she knew, and would soon want to know what was wrong.

When she opened the door, it was Jack, and not her father, who sat at the large, antique desk by the window. He was wearing a beige, light-weight business suit, but had already removed the jacket and tie which were slung over the back of his chair, and had opened the two, top buttons of his shirt.

'Oh, it's you,' she managed to get out.

Nicky's heart lurched painfully as he looked at her.

'Good-morning, Nicky,' he replied. His voice, cold as the ocean floor, was only matched by the shards of ice-blue which were his eyes.

'Do you know where I can find Pops?' she asked, trying to mask her trembling.

He moved his lips in a caricature of a smile which didn't reach his eyes.

'Yes, he's gone to Holetown. He won't be back until this evening. Why do you ask?'

Nicky looked down at the floor, unable to meet his gaze.

'We . . . we were going to work on next year's pricing structure together.'

He closed the book he had been working on.

'OK, we'll start on it now.'

Her eyes flew to his in horror.

'You and me? Now?'

This was something she hadn't envisaged, having to work with him. It was one thing to see him around, but quite another to have to spend any amount of time working with him. Her heart sank.

'Yes, why not?' He stood up and came around the desk towards her. 'If you remember, I am now a partner in this business.

We'll work on it together and discuss it with your father when he gets back.'

Nicky backed away from him, shaking her head.

'No, Jack,' she protested, 'really, I can't do that.'

His hand shot out to grab her arm and Nicky felt his touch scorching her skin.

'Yes, Nicky, really, you can,' he drawled, steering her towards a vacant chair and forcing her down in it. He pushed a pen and a pad in front of her. 'Here you are, start.'

Nicky took the pen in her fingers and, keeping her head lowered so that her hair hid her face from him, stared at the page for long minutes, seeing nothing. How could he be doing this to her, forcing her to stay in his presence when he must know what a strain it was for her?

This morning, she could no more think than fly to the moon. The pain of being near him was too great to endure and she would have to leave, even if it meant admitting defeat. She looked up at him. He wasn't working either, just staring at her intently.

'What's up with you this morning?' he asked, studying her carefully, as though seeing her for the first time. 'Good grief, you look like death. What have you been doing to yourself?'

She resented his attitude.

'I may not look quite my best today, but—'

'That's an understatement, if ever I heard one. What's wrong, Nicky?'

'Nothing.'

Her bottom lip started to tremble and she clamped down on it tightly with her teeth, shaking her head. Jack watched the movement like an eagle watching its prey.

'Nothing? It sure looks like a lot of something to me.' He stared at her for a while and Nicky became increasingly disturbed by his closeness. 'This is all about last night, isn't it?' he said at last.

She nodded, reluctantly. Jack sighed.

'Nicky, you brought that on yourself. There's no-one to blame but you,' he said quietly.

The gentleness of his tone was her undoing, and tears began to fall as sobs racked her body. He groaned and pulled her to him.

'Don't cry, darling, please, don't cry.'

His mouth came down to her face, with warm kisses to dry her hot tears. Nicky hated herself for wanting his touch, but it was a balm to her bruised soul.

'Nicky, can't you trust me?'

The telephone ringing cut abruptly across his words and he swore before reaching for it. Nicky mopped at her tears with a handkerchief and, standing up, headed towards the door. Jack put a hand over the receiver.

'Nicky, wait.'

She glanced at him briefly, shaking her head

in reply to his command before walking out of the office and closing the door quietly behind her.

She made her way back to her cottage, avoiding the well-frequented places as far as possible, anxious not to run into any of the guests in her distressed state. Once inside, she threw herself on her bed. What was the point of going on with this? She rolled over on to her back.

She had to face facts. Jack had Emerald, so there was no chance of him being serious about her. Admittedly, he was unable to keep his hands off her when they were together, but she was probably no more than a passing fancy to him.

What made it so upsetting was that in different circumstances, Nicky could have liked Emerald. She appeared to have a good sense of humour and might have been fun to know. Well, there was no point moping, she concluded. There was only one thing to do. When the going gets tough, the tough go shopping, her mother used to say. Her work was up-to-date now, so she decided to take the rest of the day off and go into Bridgetown for some window-shopping.

But her shopping expedition was no more successful than the start of her day had been, and she returned to the hotel that evening with unwanted purchases which she had been talked into by a persuasive assistant while her own thoughts had been miles away.

*   *   *

At the end of the week, the hotel held a buffet under the stars for the guests. It was always a popular evening and guests from other hotels often came to join in the musical entertainment that was laid on.

Nicky was circulating, chatting to people from the hotel, making sure they were enjoying themselves. She had noticed a young man watching her all evening, putting away copious amounts of alcohol. She didn't recognise him as one of the hotel's own guests and this was confirmed when he approached her.

'I wonder if you could help me,' he asked, swaying slightly.

Nicky put a polite smile on her face.

'I'll do my best,' she replied.

'Well, I seem to have misplaced my car keys. I think I must have dropped them in the carpark.' He sniggered. 'Do you think you could help me look for them?'

She looked at the man, who couldn't have been more than her own age, and saw that he was in no state to drive.

'Perhaps I could call you a cab, sir,' she said. 'I think perhaps that might be better than you driving back to your hotel tonight.'

He rocked backwards on his heels and

96

pretended to consider this.

'Good idea. But could we look for the keys first? I don't want to lose them.'

This sounded reasonable to Nicky, who knew what a nuisance it could be, getting replacement keys for guests who had lost theirs.

'OK. Let's go have a look,' she said, indicating the way to the carpark and falling into step behind the stranger.

Once there, he didn't seem to have much idea which was his hired car, but eventually pointed to one which he thought might be it.

Nicky, trying to hold on to her temper, started to look on the ground around the car, so missed him coming up behind her until he grabbed her around the waist and threw her against the car.

The breath was knocked from her and her walkie-talkie set, which she had been holding in her hand, went spinning from her grasp to smash on the gravel. It took her a few seconds to catch her breath and come to her senses.

He pawed her body, and as she opened her mouth to scream, he covered it with his hand. He smelled of stale beer and cigarettes and Nicky felt sick.

He was now breathing heavily and Nicky pummelled away at his chest with her fists. Just when she thought he was going to back off, she heard a steel voice cut through the night air.

'If I were you, I'd leave her alone.'

97

The young man raised his head and turned towards the voice.

'Oh, really?' He sneered. 'And just who do you think you are?'

Jack walked across to them and leaned on the next car.

'It doesn't matter who I am, but I think you should know that she's under age.'

Nicky got out from the grasp of the young man and rubbed her hands over her body where he had painfully grabbed her.

'Under age?'

Startled, he looked at Nicky and then back to Jack.

'You're joking.'

'Sorry. It's true. She looks a lot older than her age, doesn't she? We're always having to rescue some poor soul from her clutches.'

Far from being thrilled with her rescuer, Nicky was incensed.

'Jack Morgan, how dare you tell—imply that I . . .'

'And she lies, of course.' He shook his head. 'Sad, isn't it? Such a beautiful, young girl, such a waste.'

He looked at the young man and shrugged his shoulders.

'Now, you look like a young man of the world. I suggest we hush this up for you. Go back to your own hotel and we'll forget all about this. Find someone more your own age.'

The young man preened under Jack's

careful smooth talking and straightened his tie.

'Right. Good idea. But I think you should take more care of her. It's a disgrace. She shouldn't be out on her own.'

Jack smiled.

'You're absolutely right. I'll certainly take more care of her from now on.'

The young man gave Nicky one last look and, taking a bunch of keys out of his pocket, got into the car, started the engine and reversed out of the carpark.

He leaned out of his car window, and shouted, 'You should be locked up!' and roared off into the night.

'He's right you know, Nicky,' Jack said. 'You aren't safe out on your own. Is it any wonder he jumped you? Look at you. What, exactly, do you call that thing you are wearing?'

She looked down at her dress, a diaphanous confection of many-layered, gold chiffon.

'What does it look like?' she said sarcastically. 'Obviously, it's a dress.'

'Not in my book, it isn't. Do you know you can practically see through it?'

Nicky looked down at the dress in dismay. It had been one of the items she had bought on her disastrous shopping trip to Bridgetown.

'But it's got layers and layers of material! You can't possibly see through it.'

He raised an eyebrow. 'No? Let's put that to the test, shall we? You're not wearing a bra.'

She groaned.

The assistant had told her the dress looked alluring but still left a lot to the imagination. Obviously not enough, though. That's the last time I take any notice of shop assistants, she thought bitterly!

Jack had taken her hand in his and together they started walking towards the gardens.

'What were you doing out here with him, anyway?' he asked.

'He said he'd lost his keys,' she replied, almost running to keep up with Jack.

'Then why didn't you get Joseph or one of the other members of staff to go with him? Surely you know the risk of violence against women on their own, or have you been living in a glass bowl for the past few years?' he asked, keeping up a relentless pace.

'He sounded so sensible and I thought I would be safe,' Nicky said, beginning to get out of breath. 'And I had my walkie-talkie with me!'

'You're not safe, Nicky! You're about the most dangerous woman I know.'

'Oh.'

She felt a warm glow. She liked being thought of as dangerous.

'I'm going to have to do something about you,' he said. 'I'm not prepared to spend the rest of my life rescuing you from the clutches of other men.'

'I don't need rescuing,' she said indignantly.

'Not much! You were lucky I decided to come ashore this evening,' he said, ignoring her remark.

They had reached the garden, and Jack spotted her father amongst the guests. He waved him over.

'David, I'm going to take this creature away for a while, if that's OK with you. If you need me, you know how to reach me.'

Her father looked at Nicky then back to Jack, a look of understanding passing between the two men. David smiled.

'Take as long as you like, Jack,' he said, gripping the younger man's shoulder warmly.

'Now just hang on a minute, you two, I'm not going—' Nicky began.

'Looks like you'll have your hands full, though,' David said.

Jack laughed. 'I expect I'll cope.'

'Pops, can't you . . .'

But her father had already gone, waving to her over his shoulder as he walked off. Still holding her hand, Jack pulled her in the direction of the beach.

'Well, really, that's too bad of him,' Nicky burst out, not looking where she was going and tripping over a stone on the path.

Jack dragged her across the deserted beach, dimly illuminated by the lanterns from the hotel gardens. At the jetty, he helped her into the yacht's dinghy.

'Jack,' she asked, gasping for breath, 'would you please tell me what you are doing?'

Starting the outboard engine, he headed the

little boat out into the bay.

Turning to her, he said, 'I'm doing what my instincts told me to do the first time I ever set eyes on you. I'm kidnapping you.'

CHAPTER NINE

Nicky's eye gaped in amazement. 'You can't kidnap me! I won't let you,' she said almost hysterically.

'It's too late, Nicky. I already have.'

Nicky fumed in silence. The only noise on the calm, limpid water was the comforting sound of the little boat's engine as they headed towards the yacht.

Mike was sitting in the main saloon when they boarded, and although he must have been surprised by their arrival, he didn't show it by as much as a raised eyebrow.

He had been reading and listening to music. He put down his book as they entered and smiled at them.

'A change of plan, Mike,' Jack said, bypassing the usual courtesies.

He picked up a crystal glass and poured himself a whisky. Holding it out towards Nicky he raised his eyebrows in question. She shook her head and he downed the drink in one swallow before adding another finger of amber liquid to the glass.

'I'm ready,' Mike said putting a bookmark in his book and standing up.

'Take the dinghy back to the hotel and ask David to give you a bed. I'm not sure when I'll be back, but keep an eye on him while I'm gone. Make sure he doesn't overdo it. OK?'

'Sure. No problem,' Mike replied. 'I'll just go and throw some things in a bag.'

Nicky watched him go in amazement. He hadn't asked Jack a single question just gone to do what was asked of him. If it had been Nicky, she would have asked a whole lot of questions first, she knew.

Jack finished his drink, and as he led her below, she could hear Mike, busy in his cabin, opening and closing drawers, obviously packing.

Jack opened a door, switched on some wall-lights and stood back for her to enter the cabin.

'Make yourself comfortable,' he said.

'Jack . . .'

'People who have been kidnapped don't get to ask questions,' he replied, turning on his heel and closing the door after him.

Nicky sat down angrily on the silk bedcover and looked around. Even though she was so cross with Jack, she had to admit her surroundings were beautiful. No expense had been spared on the furnishings.

Silk curtains and pillows matched the cover. The wall-lights at the head of the bed were attached to champagne-coloured panelling and the cupboards and wardrobes were all finished in maple. Downlighters in the ceiling gave a soft glow to the cabin's interior and even the dressing-table stool slid out from under its recess on a brass arm to match the wall-lights.

She sat on the bed for some time, trying to decide what to do next. She was darned if she was going out to find Jack. If he wanted her, he would have to come and get her. She wasn't about to start running after him again.

Her toes curled into the thick, beige carpet as she poked around the cupboards and wardrobes, all empty. Opening a maple door, she discovered a small but elegant shower-room, its shelves filled with toiletries and large towels.

Well, Jack had told her to make herself comfortable, so she would do just that. It would help pass the time. Undressing, she opened the opaque door to the shower and turned on the water.

As she showered, Nicky wondered what Jack had done with Emerald. Perhaps she was away for a few days and that was why Jack had arranged to bring her here tonight.

She dried herself and, searching amongst the array of bottles, found a new toothbrush. Breaking open the wrappings, she scrubbed her teeth before rinsing her underwear in the sink and folding the towels neatly again over the rail.

She slipped into bed, luxuriating in the width of it. Whatever Jack had planned, she wasn't about to be a party to it. Tomorrow morning, he would have to take her straight back ashore.

The freshly-laundered sheets did nothing to comfort her and she lay awake tossing and turning for hours before, eventually, drifting off to sleep. Sometime during the night, she surfaced just long enough to hear the throb of powerful engines, but was soon asleep again.

She awoke to the sun streaming in through the small windows of the cabin. The smell of bacon cooking made her mouth water, reminding her it had been a long time since she had eaten anything.

She got out of bed, stretching luxuriously, and looked out of the cabin window, squinting her eyes against the sun. All she could see were sky and water.

'That's funny. Where's the beach and hotel?'

She sat on the edge of her bed and thought about it, muttering to herself.

'When I am out on the swimming platform in the morning, I look back at the hotel and the sun is in my eyes. Today, the sun is in my eyes and there's no hotel. Strange.'

She pursed her lips, deep in thought. This certainly needed investigating. Pulling a face at the crumpled evening dress she had worn last night, she dragged it on over her now-dried underwear and followed the smell of food.

No-one was about. She poked her head into the galley. The mouth-watering smells were coming from the oven. Two glasses of orange juice were sitting on the counter, but there was no sign of Jack.

She walked on through the dining area, where she saw places laid for two. If Emerald was on board, perhaps she wasn't too good first thing in the morning, she knew some pregnant women weren't.

Out on the aft deck, she looked around and couldn't believe her eyes. There was nothing to see except sea and sky! She climbed the ladder to the flybridge for a better look and slowly turned a full circle. There was nothing, not even a bird flying by. Nicky felt as though she were the only person in the world.

She heard a noise down below and went through the hatch, and down the stairs to the dining area to hunt for Jack. He would have to be told he couldn't just run off with a person when he felt like it, and make them a virtual prisoner.

She found him in the galley, checking the contents of the oven. He was wearing only a pair of red shorts. Red for danger, Nicky thought, watching his muscles rippling as he moved, admiring his body in spite of herself. He was closing the oven door when he saw her.

'Good-morning, sleepy-head,' he said,

coming over to give her a resounding kiss.

His smile, as he released her, was devastating, until he spotted the dress. Nicky followed his gaze to see what was wrong. It was creased, she knew that, but there wasn't much she could do about it now.

'Don't look at me like that,' she said. 'Before I got dragged here, I didn't get a chance to pack, unlike some people. What I'm wearing now is all I have on this boat.'

'From the looks of things, you're not going to have that much longer, either,' he said, teasing her.

Nicky folded her arms across her chest.

'Oh . . . you . . . you unspeakable, arrogant . . .'

Words failed her. It was one thing to be kidnapped, but quite another to be left without a stitch of clothing! Terrified he was going to drag it off her, she turned on her heel and ran back to her cabin, slamming the door behind her, scrambling into bed and pulling the covers up over her head.

A few minutes later, the covers were unceremoniously ripped off her and a pile of clothes landed on her head. She shrieked and sat up, fighting off the garments.

'What the . . .'

'There should be something here that will do,' Jack said.

He sat down on the edge of the bed and planted a kiss on her bare shoulder. Nicky picked up a shirt and held it against her. It was certainly far more serviceable than the dress, she had to admit.

'Don't be long sorting something out. Breakfast will be ready in five minutes.'

Nicky was ready in four! Hastily, she went through the pile of clothes Jack had brought. They were all T-shirts and shirts of his, together with a few pairs of shorts. She ended up choosing a large, white cotton shirt and wore it with the sleeves rolled up over her elbows.

She did a twirl in front of the full-length mirror on the wall. The shirt only just covered her bottom, but it would have to do. Splashing on perfume, which she had found on the bathroom shelf earlier, she made her way back to the galley.

Jack was taking food out of the oven and dishing it up on to large plates. He looked at her appreciatively.

'Mmm, I'm hungry. How about you?'

Nicky had the strangest feeling that he didn't mean food, either. She put a hand up to her tousled hair, blushing.

'Well, I could eat, if not a horse, then a considerably large, small pony,' she said.

He laughed delightedly, the sound flowing over her in warm waves.

'Then a considerably large, small pony it shall be.'

They ate in companionable silence. Feeling

full of content, Nicky finally laid her fork down and wiped her mouth with a napkin.

'Jack?'

'Yes?'

'Where are we?'

'Who knows?' he said, waving a hand in the general direction of the water. 'That's the Caribbean out there. I do know that but as for the rest . . .' He shrugged his shoulders.

'But how long are we staying here?'

He poured them each coffee from a silver pot.

'As long as it takes.'

'Jack, don't be difficult.'

'I'm not being difficult, Nicky. We're staying right here until you agree to marry me.'

He looked at her steadily.

'Wh-what did you say?'

Nicky, her coffee cup halfway to her mouth, splashed the contents over the shirt she was wearing. She put down her cup and dabbed ineffectually at the growing stains while trying to get her thoughts unscrambled.

'You heard.'

'Marry you? But I can't . . . I mean, it's not possible!'

Her head was spinning with the thought of it. Marriage? To Jack? What about Emerald? Surely he couldn't have forgotten his responsibility to her?

Jack hadn't moved. He just sat gazing at her, which Nicky found unnerving.

'I shall just refuse,' she responded, unconsciously pleating the coffee-stained napkin with her fingers. 'I'm not being forced into anything. At some stage you will have to go back. You can't stay out here for ever, can you?' she parried.

'You'd better believe it,' he said. 'I can afford to stay here for as long as it takes—weeks, months, even years. Water, oil, provisions—everything I need can be delivered. I have a Fax and a satellite telephone which means I can contact any place in the world from here, so my business will continue as usual. Admittedly, if it were to be for ever I would seriously have to consider changing the boat every five or six years, but that's a minor problem.'

She looked at him, shocked.

'But why?'

'Why do people normally get married, Nicky?' he asked her quietly.

She raised her shoulders and shook her head.

'I don't know.'

'Think about it, Nicky. Take all the time you need. Think about all that's happened between us, all the things we have said to each other. When you are ready, you will know where to find me.'

'But Jack . . .'

He was already on his feet, clearing away the breakfast dishes and Nicky knew it would be useless to ask him anything now. She helped him carry them to the galley where he stacked them in the dishwasher.

'I'll have to go and work for a few hours,' he said when they had finished, 'but make yourself at home. There are plenty of books and magazines around, and the radio. I don't think we can pick up any television channels out here, but you could try.'

He went down to his office, and as she passed his door some time later, she could hear the sound of the Fax machine chattering away.

Nicky spent long hours doing nothing but thinking. She took his advice and turned over every conversation they had ever had, re-lived every minute they had spent together.

*   *   *

Jack continued to be charming and treated her as a well-loved guest, making sure she had everything she wanted. They spent time together talking about most things except the reason for her being on the yacht.

They cooked together, swam together, ate together, sunbathed together—but each night she went to her cabin and he went to his, deliberately keeping her at arms' length.

The nights were the worst. Nicky lay in bed unable to sleep, looking at the same problems from different angles. There was no question in her mind that she loved him, and although Jack had never said he loved her, by his actions, she knew he was fond of her. Good marriages had been built on less than that, hadn't they?

Besides, they were good together. The sticking point was always Emerald. If only she knew what Jack felt about the situation it might help with her decision, but she realised he wasn't about to discuss it with her.

If only she could trust him. Trust—there was that word again. She sat up in bed and looked into the darkness, hugging her knees under the covers.

Her father trusted Jack, she knew. Passing Jack's office door that morning, Nicky had heard Jack talking to her father, and they had been laughing about something. Her father always said he could spot a fraud, yet he had trusted Jack with her. Trusted him enough to let Jack bring her away, not knowing how long she would be or where he was taking her.

And Mike—he was the same. He hadn't even questioned Jack when he had been asked to leave the yacht and go to the hotel. At the time, Nicky had put it down to the fact that Mike had known him for many years, but she knew that was not really relevant. Mike simply trusted him, and so did she.

This simple truth settled on Nicky as gently as dove's wings. She knew Jack was an honest man. He would never hurt anyone if he could help it. Whatever had happened between him and Emerald, she knew he would do what was right. Trusting Jack might be like running towards a cliff edge and not stopping, but Nicky knew that, as long as he was holding her hand, she had nothing to worry about.

Switching on the bedside lamp, she looked at the clock. Three in the morning! She would have to wait until dawn before telling Jack. Bouncing out of bed, she paced the confines of the small cabin for what seemed like hours before crawling back into bed and falling asleep almost immediately.

The next morning, she slept late. Hardly having patience for a shower, she pulled on a shirt and a pair of Jack's shorts fastened with one of his leather belts and raced for the deck. She found Jack on the flybridge, sunbathing.

'Jack! Jack!' she shouted, coming to kneel down at the side of his cushions.

He opened one eye and peered at her.

'Where's the fire?'

'It's far more serious than that,' Nicky said, dropping a pert kiss on the end of his nose.

'Oh, no, we're sinking!'

He groaned, putting a hand to his head in mock horror. She laughed.

'No, nothing like that. Jack, I'm going to marry you,' she blurted out.

He sat up abruptly, his eyes searching her face. He didn't speak for a long time and Nicky began to think he might have changed

113

his mind. Then he pulled her to him, lowered his mouth to hers, his kiss deep and satisfying and it was a long time before he put her away from him.

'Nicky, you told me once that you would always be honest with me. You said I might not like what you said, but that it would always be the truth as you saw it.'

She nodded, remembering when she had told him.

'Darling, I have to ask you.' His voice sounded rough with emotion. 'Why are you marrying me?'

Nicky looked into his eyes and saw all the love he felt for her shining in their depths—all his hopes and fears in two pools of blue. His smile was gentle.

'Because I love you, Jack.' She took a deep breath. 'And because I trust you.'

'Thank goodness,' he breathed, pulling her towards him and burying his face in her hair.

She wrapped her arms around him and held him tight, revelling in their closeness. He rained kisses on her with a fierceness which surprised and delighted Nicky making her aware of how much he needed her.

Much later, Jack opened the fridge in the bar unit and took out two chilled glasses and a bottle of champagne. Popping the cork, he poured the golden bubbles and brought them back to where Nicky was sitting.

'Champagne for breakfast. Wow!' she said.

'Sweetheart, if you want champagne for breakfast every day of your life, you shall have it.'

She looked at him archly over the top of her glass.

'Bit of a coincidence, wasn't it, having this in the fridge?'

'Of course not. As I've told you before, it's just good management and forward planning.' He grinned.

'And just how forward was your planning?'

He pretended to think about it.

'Oh, it's been in here since the day we spent going around the island together,' he replied.

Nicky was astonished, and said as much.

'Why that day in particular?' she wanted to know.

'Because that day, my darling, was the day I knew, for sure, that I was in love with you.'

Her heart filled to overflowing with love for him. She hadn't been wrong to trust him.

'But now,' he said, 'I think it's time we got the problem of Emerald out of the way.'

Nicky's face fell.

'Jack, I don't think it's a subject I ought to be discussing with you. Whatever you decide to do is OK with me,' she declared.

He put down his glass and took her face in his hands.

Looking down at her, he said, 'You never did get it, did you?'

'Get what?'

115

'Emerald—she's my sister.'

'What?' she burst out, unable to take in what Jack was saying.

'Watch my mouth, Nicky, and I'll say it again. Emerald is my sister.'

'But she's Mike's sister.'

'Oh? Did Mike or Emerald tell you that?'

'No, but—'

'Did you ask them?'

'No, but—'

'Then how did you come to that conclusion?'

She lowered her head and bit on her bottom lip, worrying it with her teeth.

'I've been very stupid, haven't I?' she said finally.

Jack wrapped his arms around her.

'No, my darling. You've been exasperating, adorable, unbelievably maddening and loveable, but never stupid.'

'Why didn't somebody tell me?'

He settled her comfortably in the curve of his arm.

'Does the name Jordan Matheson mean anything to you?'

Nicky shook her head.

'He is an internationally-known financier, rich as Croesus, who also happens to be married to Emerald. They live in Hong Kong and had been living there quite happily until she started the baby. Jordan, poor soul, has gone right over the top with excitement and says he wants to retire to watch his son and heir grow up.'

'But that's quite understandable, Jack, isn't it?' Nicky asked, who thought it would be lovely to have a child of her own and watch it grow up.

'Of course it is, but not when you have as many fingers in pies as Jordan has in Hong Kong. Nothing will do but for them to move, lock, stock and barrel, back to the islands. There is a business which he hopes to get involved in over here, and he asked me to start the preliminary negotiations for it, so no-one would know he was going to be involved.'

'Because it would put the price up?' Nicky guessed.

'Exactly. Also, he wanted to sell his holdings in the companies over there before he moved back, but if the financial community had got wind of this, the price he could get would be considerably lower than he hoped. Also, Emerald decided to come over and look for a house before her pregnancy gets too advanced and while she can still get round easily.'

'Oh, I see,' Nicky said. 'So she was staying on the boat rather than a hotel to keep a low profile? Is that why Mike didn't want me to meet Emerald?'

'Precisely, my darling. Who said women aren't intelligent?' he teased. 'Of course, Mike hadn't had the advantage of knowing you like I did, or he wouldn't have been worried. We had heard that a reporter, working undercover at a local hotel, was on the look-out for her even before she arrived. At one stage, Mike and I were convinced it was you.'

'Well, really! What a cheek,' Nicky said indignantly.

'That was the day of your accident, remember, and you didn't tell Mike or me who you were. When you got into difficulties on the raft, I thought you were a reporter setting me up. Someone who had got wind of what was going on and was trying to get more information.

'In fact, in the evening, you were trying to get me thrown out of the hotel and I convinced myself that it was because your cover had been blown and you had a guilty conscience. I was totally besotted by then, anyway. When I discovered who you were and saw what a feisty, little madam you were, I just knew I had to have you.'

She pulled away, and looked up at him, frowning.

'But, Jack, when you decided, so suddenly, to change your mind and go into partnership with Pops instead, wasn't it a bit dangerous, putting all that money into the hotel's account the very next day?'

He laughed.

'Not in the least. I was desperate for your father to start spending it. I didn't want you talking him out of the deal just when I had found you.'

Nicky smiled smugly, cuddling closer to him.

'I wanted to tell you. about Emerald that night I took a soaking, but I had given my word to Jordan that I wouldn't discuss her visit with anyone to avoid the financial papers getting wind of it. It was the nearest I've ever come to breaking my word.'

Kissing the top of her head, he went on, 'When it was possible for me to tell you, I couldn't. I knew I wanted to marry you and spend the rest of my life with you but I didn't know how you felt about me, so I had to persuade you to tell me.'

'Huh! Some persuasion,' Nicky retorted, thinking about how she had spent the past few days, and glad that the misunderstandings were all behind them.

She ran her finger over Jack's chest.

'If you don't stop doing that, I won't be responsible for my actions,' he said huskily.

She giggled and whispered, 'Goody.'

'I don't need a better invitation than that,' he responded, standing up and pulling her to her feet.

'Jack,' she said seriously, wrapping her arms around his neck and gazing up at him, 'I've wasted an awful lot of time, haven't I?'

'Definitely.' He grinned, returning her kiss. 'In fact, I think we'll have to get started right away on making it up. I can see that it could take quite a while.'

They picked up the glasses and the bottle of champagne and made their way down to Jack's stateroom. As they passed the door to his office, the phone started to ring.

Nicky glanced at him and raised her eyebrows, questioningly. He shook his head and pulled the door closed.

'The rest of the world will have to wait.'